ANA'S ASTEROID

M.K. HUTCHINS

IMMORTAL WORKS
SALT LAKE CITY

Immortal Works LLC
1505 Glenrose Drive
Salt Lake City, Utah 84104
Tel: (385) 202-0116

Cover Art by Rebecca Barney
barneydesign.com

This book is a work of fiction. Names, characters, businesses, organizations, places, events and incidents either are the product of the author's imagination or are used fictitiously. Any resemblance to actual persons, living or dead, events, or locales is entirely coincidental.

ISBN 978-1-953491-44-2 (Paperback)
ASIN B0BFVSJ7CM (Kindle Edition)

To my dad, who taught me how to look through a telescope.

CHAPTER 1

I raced Cornelius home after school through the corridors of the *Platinum Phoenix*. He took the right-hand side, and I took the left. The dents in stainless steel walls made our reflections wobble.

"I'll beat you this time!" Cornelius called from behind. He was eleven—two years younger than me.

I laughed. "I doubt—"

But my feet slipped out from under me. I skidded across the floor. Like all the other kids on this asteroid mining colony, my clothes were sewn from surplus mylar blankets—slick stuff. I crashed into a sealed-off door. There were plenty of unused corridors like that, leftover from better days when the *Platinum Phoenix* actually had passengers.

Cornelius laughed and sped past me, his legs pumping fast. I picked myself up and jogged after him.

He waited for me at our door, red-faced and panting. "Told you, Ana. I'm getting faster."

I rolled my eyes. "Or I *fell*."

That didn't dampen his round-faced grin in the slightest. "I still won."

I palmed the keypad, and our door swished open to the side.

"Hey, Mom!" I called. "We're home!"

No one answered. I stepped in. The front room of our apartment—a steel kitchen table, sagging couch, and one armchair—was empty. I peeked into our parents' room. Nobody.

"Weird," Cornelius said, voicing my own thoughts. Mom had been putting in plenty of overtime at the In-Situ Resource Utilization—or ISRU—refineries. But she always scheduled her shifts so she'd be here when we got home, even if she collapsed and fell asleep ten minutes later. Dad was at the school. As the only teacher on the *Platinum Phoenix*, he usually stayed late.

"Maybe she fell asleep at her desk again," I offered. Without her weary smile, our apartment felt like a sterile, metallic box.

I ducked into my room to check on Leonhart, my succulent plant. A little lamp shone on him. No windows for us; the colony was built a kilometer under the surface of our massive asteroid.

I drank in the greenness of him, the beautiful radial symmetry of his leaves. "One day, somehow," I whispered, "I'm going to save up a small fortune and buy us a ticket to Earth, where there are *continents* full of grass and trees. Let's go be botanists together, okay?"

"Are you talking to your plant again?" Cornelius called.

My cheeks heated. "It's called *science!* Talking to your plants is proven to help them grow better."

"You only looked up that study after you started talking to it."

I stroked one of Leonhart's smooth, thick leaves and lowered my voice even more. "Cornelius is just jealous."

"I heard that!" He paused, his tone switching from teasing to hopeful in a heartbeat. "Hey, want to play *Racing All-Stars Unleashed?*"

I wanted to stare at the Mendel Academy for Young Botanists website and the panorama of its lush campus, covered in purple jacaranda trees and flowering mounds of rhododendrons. Or its photos of students in the Pampas near Rio Grande do Sul, doing botanical surveys surrounded by oceans of grass. My parents had grown up in that paradise of green. I still wasn't sure how they could choose to leave it behind.

But Cornelius would tease me if I said I'd rather stare at pictures of a school. "I should do my homework first."

"You always do your homework first."

"That way I'll have plenty of time to play *Racing All-Stars* with you later."

Cornelius snorted. "You mean then you'll have *no* time to do anything but obsess over your biology paper."

I ignored him, sat at the desk under my loft bed, and edited my report to the muted background noise of jet-propelled race cars.

An hour passed. Then another. With bleary eyes and a rumbling stomach, I tried to reread my paper for the thousandth time. I couldn't find anything else to fix. Either it was flawless, or my brain had quit. I wandered out to the couch and sat by Cornelius. "I...guess I could play now."

He looked worried instead of thrilled. "Do you think we should call Mom or Dad or something?"

It wasn't like either of them to be out this late. I tapped my wristlet. A tiny bulb on its side projected text across the silvery sleeve of my mylar shirt; the auto-stabilizing software kept the words from wobbling as I scrolled through my inbox. Neither of my parents had sent me a message.

My finger hovered over the call button. Surely, nothing was wrong. I'd call, and they'd both apologize about getting caught up in some boring meeting.

The door swished open. Mom and Dad walked in, carrying foil-wrapped trays from food processing.

"Supper," Mom said, in a voice deader than the abandoned moons of Mars. The purple-black circles under her eyes seemed darker than usual. Dad wasn't any cheerier.

Cold dread clenched around my lungs. "What's wrong?"

Dad ran a hand through his thinning hair and said nothing. Mom managed a weak smile and arranged the trays on the table. "I'm sorry we're both so late. You must be starving."

We were on tight rations these days, but for the first time in a month, I wasn't eager to tear into my food. Cornelius didn't share my hesitation—he ripped open the top piece of foil, letting out a puff of steam that smelled like old socks. Beneath, peas and amaranth swam in a gray-green sauce of algae and nutritional yeast.

My parents nibbled at their meals, not talking.

"What broke this time?" I asked. "The navigational thrusters?"

I couldn't think of much that hadn't broken. The fabricator —a sophisticated 3D printer—had been down for six months. The water recycler sputtered out next. Technicians patched it together, but it ran at seventy percent efficiency without exact, fabricated replacement parts. The aeroponics garden used to grow strawberries. Not anymore.

After that, the air scrubbers needed a patch-up job. Then the furnace.

My parents looked at each other, silently debating how much they ought to say.

"If you don't tell me, I'm going to assume that the air scrubbers failed completely, and we'll all suffocate tomorrow."

I expected them to laugh. But the worry lines around their mouths deepened. They squeezed each other's hands. In a soft voice my father said, "It's not...not *quite* that bad."

A black hole of worry imploded in my stomach. Cornelius studied our parents' reactions as he chewed.

Dad sighed. "Do you want me to tell them? I can do it."

Mom hesitated, then nodded. I couldn't tell if she honestly thought this was a good idea or if she couldn't muster the energy to disagree. She bent her head over her plate, picking out a few peas, not looking at us.

Dad cleared his throat. "The last of the repair robots for the mining equipment broke last week. Today, both charge-setter machines leaked blasting gel all over themselves. Without the robots, we have no way to clean up the mess. Mining operations have stopped completely."

Cornelius swallowed. "That doesn't sound so bad."

I knew exactly how bad that was. The *Platinum Phoenix* didn't just mine heavy metals to sell to Earth once our massive asteroid orbited back around to the planet. We mined ice, too. Ice could be melted for drinking water—or chemically split into breathable oxygen and hydrogen fuel to heat the colony.

With the water recycler, air scrubbers, and furnace all patched up and running less-than-perfectly, we needed every bit of ice we could get.

"Can you and the other ISRU technicians fix the repair bots?" I asked Mom.

Mom rubbed her bloodshot eyes. "We're...working on it."

It didn't sound like they were succeeding.

"How long do we have?" I asked, not sure I wanted to hear the answer.

"Maybe we'll find a way to fix them." She tried to sound reassuring, but her voice was thin and exhausted.

"How long?" I asked again.

Mom sighed and set down her fork. "A week. We'll run out of air in a week if we don't figure this out."

I'd just been joking about suffocating, but her words still felt surreal. Distant. Untrue. Our family—and the six hundred other inhabitants of the *Platinum Phoenix*—couldn't just cease to exist, especially over some mining equipment. Cornelius glanced at me, like I could say something to make it better.

"Not all parents will choose to tell their children about this,"

Dad cut in. "Please honor their decision and don't spread this around at school."

"School?" I spluttered. "You want us to go to school when we're all about to die?"

"School tomorrow, like normal," Dad said firmly. "Eat your dinner, Ana."

CHAPTER 2

I knew better than to waste food—there wasn't exactly extra hanging around in a cupboard somewhere. After downing every gram of dinner, I chucked my foil dish into the recycler. The sour dread in my mouth should have made everything taste horrible, but apparently, algae and nutritional yeast already taste as bad as anything can. The bile rising in my throat might have actually improved the flavor.

I lay in bed for over an hour, timing how long I could hold my breath. The first thirty seconds wasn't bad, but then a prickling feeling tightened in my lungs, and my throat swelled up.

At best, I made it to a minute and thirty-two seconds before I gasped in fresh air. I tapped on my wristlet and did a quick bit of research. I'd probably pass out after three minutes without oxygen. If Mom and the other techs didn't fix the charge-setters, I'd have a minute and twenty-eight seconds of unbearable, lung-burning agony before I suffocated.

Except...no. The air wouldn't disappear. The air scrubbers wouldn't be able to take out the carbon dioxide. We'd all be poisoned and drift off, unable to scream in the end. Was that better?

I set my wristlet on my desk next to Leonhart, turned off the light, and tried to sleep. My dreams weren't any less morbid than my thoughts before bed. I woke up to sore muscles and a pounding headache behind my eyes, like I hadn't slept at all.

School. How was I supposed to sit through school today?

CLASSES TOOK place in another stainless steel cube of a room, though Dad had covered up some of the walls with colorful maps, number lines, and a periodic table of the elements. About forty kids, most older than me, sat at the various round tables. The youngest child, a four-year-old, played with blocks while the teens modeled chemistry equations.

Zoe, my best friend, waved cheerfully at me. I tried to mirror her expression, but smiling made me nauseous. I sat across the table from her and pulled up my independent school work on my bar comp.

Dad managed to act normal—helping a younger kid load their virtual field trip before crossing the room to answer a question about Lewis dot structures. I stared blankly at my screen for an hour, failing to read even the first paragraph of my history assignment.

After that, everyone put their bar comps away for language practice. The *Platinum Phoenix* had expected most of its passengers to speak Portuguese, English, or Korean, so all the adults spoke at least one of those. Despite the lack of passengers, Dad wanted his students conversant in all three.

Then it was time for student projects. A few months ago, I'd been growing succulents—all offshoots of Leonhart—in different soil, light, and water configurations. But then the whole water-scarcity thing happened, and my lovely inedible plants didn't qualify for "essential water usage." I tried to argue that plants are good for air quality, but using the water as fuel for the recyclers was more efficient than whatever good my little garden provided.

The water conservation technicians had wanted to recycle

Leonhart too. Dad scrambled to get a note from Dr. Almeida—a medical doctor—saying that taking my plant away would be bad for my emotional and mental well-being. I'm pretty sure that made Leonhart the first service plant.

Still, I stared at the empty shelf where those succulents once sat in neat rows, each under its own light. The cheerful lights were gone too, disassembled for wires to repair more vital equipment. The closest I could get to my scrapped botany experiments was writing reports.

Zoe elbowed me. "Hey, I'm sure you'll be able to start your garden up again after we swing by Earth and buy parts to repair the fabricator. Then you'll have *two* sets of data. That's even better, right?"

Trying to smile made my face hurt. "Yeah, I guess so."

"Wow! I thought insulting your plants would wake you up. You must be *exhausted* if you can't even glare at me for that one."

"I...guess I am," I fumbled, throat tight. It was one thing for Dad to tell me what was happening on the asteroid—I wanted to know. It was another thing to ask me to lie to my friends. To pretend everything was fine.

Zoe's smile faded. She tucked her short brown hair behind her ears. "Something's wrong, isn't it?"

Part of me wanted to gush out everything. The rest of me didn't want to make Zoe miserable.

Cornelius sat at the table next to ours. He leaned back in his chair. "Yeah, she stayed up forever last night working on her paper."

"Seriously? Ana, I'd tell you to get out more, but the only place nearby is the cold, hard vacuum of space."

I gave Cornelius a thankful glance. Though I wasn't sure if I should be offended or grateful that Zoe bought it.

"Writing papers sucks," Zoe said.

Usually, I conjured up some fake enthusiasm, but I didn't have it in me today. "I finished another one yesterday. Guess I'm not excited to start a new one."

"Good! Then you can help me." A huge grin flashed across her face.

Group work was allowed, encouraged even. Cornelius never did independent projects—he always helped his friend Dae-sung plot ways to carve out a zero-g recreation hall in the dead center of the asteroid. Their ambitious construction schemes would never, ever happen—it would be mind-bogglingly expensive and probably mess with the asteroid's stability. But Dae-sung enjoyed asking ridiculous engineering questions and making up rules for zero-g soccer. Cornelius was happy to tag along.

Jayden often joined them, but today she read on her bar-comp. Maybe her parents had told her about the robots, and she couldn't bring herself to pretend everything was all right. Maybe she just had an interesting book. With her head bent down, I couldn't see her face, just her springy black curls.

"Zoe, last time I helped you, I held your reflective foils for over two hours. I was an adjustable light stand."

"Which is still more exciting than writing a paper," she said. "C'mon."

I heartily disagreed, but today, standing around and not thinking might be a good idea. "Okay."

"Yes!" Zoe whipped her scuffed, well-worn camera out of her bag. She looked through the lens, then scanned the room, stopping on me. "Hmm. Maybe I should take some portraits today. Posing is better than holding reflectors, right?"

"Zoe, I don't think I'm up to being smiley."

Cornelius looked up from Dae-sung's elaborate map. "Yeah, she misplaced a comma last night and doesn't know what to do with herself."

Zoe rolled her eyes at both of us. "I don't care if you're scowling, Ana. It's not for some family scrapbook. It's for my website. Maybe I'll make them sepia, or we could set up back-lit silhouettes."

I raised an eyebrow, unconvinced. "I'm sure you can find a better subject."

Zoe snapped a shot.

"Hey!" I protested.

She snapped another. I whipped my back to her.

"Fine, fine. Let's find some air vents and take artsy industrial shots, then. That's about the only other thing on this asteroid to photograph. I hope my readers aren't tired of stainless steel yet."

"There's the aeroponics lab," I offered, eager for any excuse to go there. I loved the laboratory, with its warehouses of vegetables growing under lights and its swirling vats of blue-green algae—the stuff actually looked pretty when it wasn't cooked. No other place on the *Platinum Phoenix* had air that smelled humid and green.

"However much I want to tease you about plants, you're right." Zoe turned. "Hey, Mr. M! Can we go down to aeroponics?"

Dad was helping the younger kids get out chalk for an art project. They always used chalk, now. Paint required water. "I'd rather keep all the students here in class today."

So no one overheard other adults talking about our impending doom? Part of me envied the way Zoe shrugged, like Dad's words meant nothing much.

Zoe wandered the classroom, looking through her camera. Eventually, she settled by the little kids, taking pictures of chubby hands wrapped around thick chalk cylinders. She pulled out a silvery reflector and positioned me with it at a tilt to soften our harsh overhead lights.

She was in her element, laughing and sticking out her

tongue to get the kids to make funny faces. She clicked, clicked, clicked, taking hundreds of shots.

These could be the last photos anyone ever took of these kids. Or of anything on the *Platinum Phoenix* for that matter.

"You should get those up on your website right away," I told Zoe as she packed up her camera.

She gave me a weird look. "Got to edit them first. Why are you so eager?"

I swallowed and tried to sound casual. "I just think they're going to be great. I mean, I did my part brilliantly. My finest reflector-holding work to date."

"You're such a dork sometimes, Ana. I haven't even *looked* at them. They might all be horrible."

"Post them anyway."

CHAPTER 3

In the afternoon, Zoe and I had our IDPOP together: In-Depth Professional Opportunity Program. Really, it was a fancy way to say *job shadowing*. Students twelve and older rotated around the various parts of the *Platinum Phoenix*. Optimistic adults claimed this would help prepare us for our future careers. Pessimistic ones said the colony wasn't getting any new recruits, and we weren't getting out, so we might as well figure out what we wanted to do on this rock.

Unfortunately, we weren't in the aeroponics lab this week. Zoe and I trudged into navigation. Sampaio and Stewart, as always, shooed us into a spare office and left us with a list of articles we'd need PhDs to understand. Usually, Zoe and I ignored their assignments and played games, read books, or talked. But I pretended I felt guilty about not working on a new biology paper and tried to read what they'd left for us. Wading through jargon I didn't understand was easier than lying and smiling at Zoe for two more hours. She snorted, plugged in her earbuds, and set to work editing her photographs on her bar comp.

After that, I headed back to the school to pick up Cornelius and finally went home where I didn't have to lie or pretend anymore.

Mom came home late again. Cornelius was in bed, though I could hear the peppy sound effects of whatever game he was playing on his wristlet. Dad sat in his room planning a history lesson, which left me free to grab Mom and drag her to the couch next to me.

"Tell me," I demanded.

She stretched her head from side to side, popping little bones in her neck. "We're close to fixing the repair robots."

"How close?"

"If everything goes smoothly, we'll boot them up tomorrow."

Nothing ever went smoothly on this asteroid, but neither of us said that aloud. I fetched her foil-wrapped dinner for her, then I disappeared into my room.

Nightmares of a creeping, suffocating death left me panting and gasping for breath when I woke up.

I hated every second of it, but I managed to get through another day of school without blurting out the truth.

Mom came home even later that night; Cornelius was already asleep.

"Ana, don't—" Dad began as soon as the door slid open.

But I ignored him and dragged Mom to the couch again. "Tell me."

Mom finger-combed her hair out of her eyes. When she exhaled, her breath shuddered like she was a broken air vent. "We fried the repair robots. But...but it might be all right. Tomorrow we're turning one of the charge-setters back on."

"With leaked blasting gel still all over the machine?" I stared at her. "Won't that make it, I dunno, *blow up?*"

"Talk nicely to your mother," Dad grumbled. He glanced at

Mom with something like envy. She could work on this problem. He couldn't. But being able to work on it didn't mean anyone could fix it.

"Perhaps if we're careful, we can operate the machine without igniting the blasting gel. Start mining again," Mom said. "That's the hope, at least."

Maybe they'd run out of ideas.

"I'm not going to school tomorrow."

Dad gave me his seriously disappointed frown. "Ana, we will continue onward—"

"I'm not going! I *hate* lying to Zoe! If these are my last days, I don't want to spend them in a classroom pretending that it matters if I understand Nezahualcoyotl's poetry or not!"

I expected Dad to double down, to lecture me on the importance of education or perseverance or something. "Do you really want to frighten Cornelius like that?"

My stomach tightened. Cornelius still mattered. "No, I don't." But I absolutely wasn't going. I softened my tone. "I'll pretend to be sick, all right? A cold or something. You can tell him I threw up if it helps."

It wasn't uncommon to come down with asteroid crud, especially on reduced rations. No one was feeling their best.

Mom nodded. "You can stay, Ana."

I SLEPT IN. When I woke, only the eerie whine of the ventilation system greeted me. My footsteps sounded too loud without the music from Cornelius' game covering them. I grabbed an algae smoothie from the fridge and slurped it down.

As I sat at our quiet, empty table, all my nightmarish thoughts came back to me. I couldn't stand being at school, but I couldn't sit here all day either. So, I tossed the empty algae foil into the recycler and headed to aeroponics.

The doors hissed open, bringing a breath of warm, wet air. Three huge glass screens hung in the front of the room, two with bar-comps attached, projecting data and pictures all over. Beyond them stood the swirling, blue-green algae tanks—vibrant and beautiful if you didn't think about what they tasted like. Past those stretched rows and rows of shelves, each housing drawers of plants under buttery yellow lights. Nowhere else on the asteroid was this alive.

Dr. Fletcher strode to the door, hands casually tucked into her lab coat pockets, blonde hair tied up in its usually messy bun. It was somehow comforting that, with everything else falling apart, Dr. Fletcher still looked like herself. "Ah, Ana. Is there something I can help you with?"

"Could I just sit in here today? With the plants?" My stomach squirmed, even though I expected she'd say yes. Dr. Fletcher was always super nice when I had IDPOP here—she actually let me help.

The pleasant expression on her face sagged. "You know, then?"

I nodded.

She squeezed my shoulder. "I'm sorry. The adults chose to come here, but you and the other kids? You were just unlucky enough to be born here. You all deserve better." She shook her head. "Of course you can stay. Stay as long as you want to, Ana."

DR. FLETCHER DIDN'T HAVE any IDPOP students, so I spent most of the day there, breathing in the greenness. I left a few minutes before school got out to beat Cornelius home and make a good show of being sick.

That night, Mom arrived home later than ever. As soon as I heard the door open, I slipped out to the front room. Cornelius wasn't sleeping yet—muffled through the wall, his bed creaked as he tossed and turned.

"Mom, I want to know—" I started.

She nodded and waved me toward the couch. Dad joined us. But Mom didn't speak. I chewed the inside of my lip and studied the shadows hanging in the crescent moons under her weary eyes. She didn't look like she'd had an encouraging day.

"Natalia?" Dad prompted.

Mom exhaled through her nose. "Is there anything to drink?"

I ran and fetched her a foil pouch of water from the fridge. She took small sips like this was the last bit of water on the ship.

"Did it work?" Dad asked the only question that mattered.

"We got one of the two charge-setters started." Mom turned the foil over in her hands. "It exploded. Destroyed itself and collapsed one of the three shafts up to the mines."

The words turned the knob of hope in my gut into a pile of shattered glass. The techs had failed. "Oh."

"Everyone...everyone on my team is going to get some rest tonight. Some real rest. Then we're going to solve this problem, long before we run out of air."

They only had four days left. "How?"

Mom plastered on a smile, hugged me, and didn't answer. She didn't know.

I HOLED up in my room after that. Ignoring my homework, I sat and stared at Leonhart, willing him to make enough oxygen to save us. I knew the two of us never had a chance of buying a ticket to Earth and attending Mendel Academy, but it would have been nice. Flowers. Grass. Water. Air.

The last time our orbit neared Earth, only a few people could afford a shuttle lift off the asteroid—my friend Manoela and her mom among them. After watching her leave, I'd cried alone in my room, angry and jealous. The jealousy remained, but the anger was gone. Now I was glad she'd managed to get off.

I pulled myself through the routine of getting ready for bed, not that I could sleep. It was past 1:00 a.m. colony-time when my door opened. Cornelius scuttled inside, his round face lit only by his wristlet. "Ana? Are you awake?"

"Yeah." I rubbed the back of my neck. "Lights."

They flickered on, revealing a red-eyed Cornelius. He climbed up the ladder and sat on the bed next to me. "For the first time in my life, I wish I'd done more homework."

For the first time in my life, I hadn't touched mine at all.

"I don't understand what's happening," Cornelius whimpered.

I nodded. Knowing *how* we were all about to die wouldn't change the fact, but I could at least explain it to him. "There's only one charge-setter left, and it's covered in leaked blasting gel, so we can't mine with it. No mining means no ice, so we can't get more water, air, or fuel. Which we need, given how broken down this colony is."

"I know that. But why don't they just send someone up into the mines to clean the charge-setter?"

"I'll show you." I twisted my wristlet to project at the wall, then I brought up a map of our asteroid—a roughly circular shape about thirty-two kilometers across. Nestled safely away from solar radiation a full kilometer under the surface, the picture showed squiggly lines crisscrossing each other like spaghetti. One line reached down toward the surface and a much smaller blob—the landing bay.

"Here's our colony, the *Platinum Phoenix*."

Cornelius nodded.

I tapped my wristlet again, and a red blob appeared a kilometer out from the colony and three and a half kilometers beneath the surface. "Here's where the best ore deposits are. Drilling a two and a half kilometer, straight shaft is super hard—time-consuming, expensive, prone to tilt and curve. You name it. The engineers drilled three access shafts at different points—each just wide enough to send up repair robots. These robots assembled all the larger machinery, piece by piece, up in the mines."

Cornelius hopped off the bed and walked over to the wall. The projection rippled across his back. He stepped to the side and traced the three thin lines leading up into the mines. "They made these shafts too small for people?"

"No one thought we'd need people. It was safer to send robots to do all the maintenance work up there."

"It's not safer now. You're sure none of the technicians would fit?" Cornelius' voice went soft and shaky—worse than when Dad called on him in class to solve a division problem he didn't know.

"Wristlet, project a to-scale image of the lift cage." A rectangular shape appeared on the wall. "This is what the repair robots ride in, like an elevator. It carries ore and ice down, too."

Cornelius frowned at the image. "Maybe someone really skinny would fit if they made it taller."

"Six years ago, they tried taller cages to speed up ore delivery. They always got caught on slight curves in the shaft. The cages *crumpled*."

Cornelius winced. "You're sure?"

I paused, tilting my head to the side. The outline of the cage almost framed him. "Can you step a little to the left? Sorry, my left."

I chewed my lip. The outline of the cage was maybe fifteen

centimeters taller than Cornelius. Ten centimeters or so taller than me. And barely wide enough for a kid to fit.

None of the adults on the *Platinum Phoenix* could travel up the shaft and into the mines. But I could.

CHAPTER 4

The *Platinum Phoenix* was supposed to be the most lucrative investment of the millennium. Nuclear engines spun asteroid 1036 Ganymed to have Earth-like gravity in the colony, then pushed the asteroid into an elliptical orbit that passed by Earth, then Mars, and back again in a little over two years. Our colony could ferry settlers and scientists to Mars, using only limited fuel to keep the asteroid in the right orbit. In the meantime, we could mine valuable metals to sell.

With life expectancy pushing one hundred and two on Earth, there had been plenty of older folks—platinums—who wanted to retire on Mars. Unlike the Moon, Mars' gravity was strong enough to avoid the bad side effects of living in low-g for a long time. Mars' gravity would be like living in a swimming pool: less joint aches, pains, and stress.

Our asteroid used to have corporate sponsors, grants, everything. I was born on the *Platinum Phoenix* into what my parents thought was a bright future.

Then the Interplanetary Commission canceled the half-built space elevator over some political spat. We couldn't get platinums into space. When I was seven, we brought the last scientists on the Mars base back to Earth.

No passengers. No more scientists. No sponsorships. Greatly reduced profits. The last time we passed by Earth, the colony could only afford basic supplies. A few people left, but most people stayed, even if they could afford a shuttle ticket.

The founders of the colony still largely believed we could subsist on mining alone. No one had seemed worried about surviving our twenty-five-month orbit, but no one had planned on the fabricator breaking beyond repair.

Which was why I found myself sitting with my parents in front of Governor Cardoso to discuss my plan for saving the *Platinum Phoenix*. We were still eight months and millions of kilometers away from Earth and anyone else who might help us. I was his only option. I wiped my clammy hands on my upcycled mylar pants.

"Your daughter, Miss Martins, sent me an interesting message late last night." He folded his hands on the cold stainless steel desk between us. It was the same color as his hair.

My throat became a desert. I had hoped the governor would just send me without telling my parents. I didn't want them to worry.

Or to say no.

He pushed a bar-comp attached to a glass screen across the desk to them. "If you'd sign this consent form."

Mom and Dad glanced at me, then furrowed their brows over the document.

"You...you want to send her up?" Dad asked.

"Her idea. Not mine." Governor Cardoso's hard, unflinching voice would have been scary in other circumstances, but right then, I needed his resolve.

"She's too young to do something so risky, so..." Mom fumbled for the right words to excuse me.

"Actually, I've contacted Dr. Almeida," Governor Cardoso said. "She assured me that Ana is, in fact, exactly young enough. She's the oldest child on this asteroid who is physically small enough to make the trip."

Fear swirled across my parents' faces. Dad sat closest to me.

He grabbed my hand and squeezed it. Hard. "You can't have our daughter."

"I volunteered!" I protested, my voice shriller than I'd planned.

"That doesn't make it right to endanger you," Dad asserted.

I tried to give my voice the same firm edge that Governor Cardoso's had. "If I don't go, I'm dead anyway. Me, you, Mom, Cornelius. And everyone else we know."

They couldn't deny that, but they pursed their lips into flat lines.

"Please, let me try," I whispered.

My parents hesitated. Their hands trembled. But they signed the consent form.

I SPENT the next day with the technicians, learning how to use a wire brush and slick orange solvent to safely scrub up blasting gel. The day after that, I got ready for the mines.

I had to wear a diaper—gross—but the suit itself was even more uncomfortable. I squeezed one foot in, then the other. The lines crisscrossing the fabric made me feel like a bottled-up tube of toothpaste, but I guess that was the point. The mines were an unpressurized vacuum. I needed the tight pressure of the suit to keep my blood from boiling.

I wormed my arms through the sleeves and my hands into the stiff gloves. A half-dozen techs checked the fit on everything. Some of them gave me grateful glances, but others had guilt squirming across their faces and wouldn't meet my eye.

Nurse Hwang took my vitals. After she gave the thumbs-up, the techs fastened an airpack to my back, then snapped on the bubble-like helmet. All the extra weight around my head made me worry I'd topple over, but I managed to walk to the airlock without swaying too much.

Dad waited for me there, all suited up with an airpack and bubble helmet. "I'm going to take you to the shaft." His voice crackled through the small speaker in my helmet. "Your mom wanted to come too, but we drew straws. She's staying with Cornelius."

Dad squeezed my hand and kept holding it like I was a little kid half my age. Just then, I didn't mind.

A twelve-minute ride up the mine shaft. A three-kilometer walk to the charge-setter. An hour or so of scrubbing it clean. Then the walk back and a twelve-minute ride home.

My airpack, with a mini air scrubber attached, could give me eight hours of breathable air—more than triple what I needed.

Dad and I stepped into the airlock, a small chamber maybe two meters by two meters. The thick aluminum and glass door clicked shut behind us, separating us from the techs and the rest of the *Platinum Phoenix*.

Air hissed, pulled through the vents. The veins on my suit seemed to squeeze tighter as pressure left the airlock.

Then the far door slid silently open. Our headlights illuminated a wide gallery of red-brown asteroid rock in front of us.

CHAPTER 5

I refused to show any fear, to linger even a step behind Dad. I strode into the gallery with him. My headlight glared on the threads of metal embedded in the smooth floor—the electromagnetic tracks of the mine carts.

Dad glanced at me. "Are you okay?"

"Of course," I replied, even though my skin prickled all over.

His long exhale rattled in the speaker. "All right then. Let's get going."

He pointed his wristlet projector toward the floor, and it illuminated the way to go. Not that there were many side passages. We walked only a minute or two before reaching the mine cart. It looked a bit like its nineteenth-century counterpart, but it was four times as big, shinier, and the computer console on the front glowed pale green. Dad boosted me over the edge, then pulled himself up. We each picked a wheel well cover to sit on.

"Technicians," Dad said. "You can start the mine cart."

It lurched forward, throwing us into the back wall. I grunted, peeling myself up into a more comfortable position. Unease burrowed into my bones as the cart sped up. Something was wrong about this place, and it wasn't just the vast darkness and the looming, rust-colored rock.

"You hurt?" Dad asked.

"No. You?"

"No."

The cart vibrated as we sped through the gallery toward the nearest of the two remaining mine shafts. That's when it struck me. I could hear myself breathe, and I could hear my Dad. But I couldn't hear anything else—not the smack when I hit the wall, or my footsteps before that, or the noise of the cart on its tracks. There wasn't any noise in a vacuum.

I slapped my hand on the floor of the cart. Nothing, of course.

Silence pressed, deep and suffocating, all around me. "So. Umm." I needed a conversation. But I had nothing to say.

"Yes?"

"I'll...umm...be back soon."

"We can turn around if you're nervous."

Of course we couldn't. We'd all die without these mines. I was the oldest kid still small enough to fit. If I didn't go, I'd just be passing on this job to Zoe or one of my other classmates. "I'm not nervous."

Gentler than it had started, the cart glided to a stop. Dad and I hauled ourselves out. In front of us stood a short, stainless steel cage dangling from pulley wires. I tried looking up the shaft, but the darkness swallowed the light from my headlamp.

Dad lowered the cage door—it hinged at the bottom, forming a short ramp. "I'll be here when you return."

"I know, Dad," I mumbled. I just wanted to hurry up and finish the mission.

"Be careful."

"I know, Dad."

Then he hugged me. "I love you."

I knew that, too.

My brain tried to hear the scrape of my boots on metal, but all remained eerily noiseless as I stepped inside. I had to bend my knees and tilt my head to fit. Dad packed my cleaning supplies and the colony's last long-comm around my feet. A regular comm couldn't cut through all this rock. My legs were already cramping.

Dad closed the door, leaving me encased in a claustrophobic metal coffin. My headlight glared over the rock dust coating the inside of the cage. A moment later, the floor pushed against the soles of my feet, and my stomach dropped. I was headed up through a tiny shaft, surrounded by kilometers and kilometers of silent, dark rock.

My elbows and knees throbbed where they pressed against the walls. Twelve minutes hadn't seemed that long before I got in here. Why hadn't I uploaded music or a book or something to my wristlet? I only had my aches and queasiness to keep me company.

I twisted my arm, managing to glance at my wristlet. I'd been in here for less than two minutes. I thought I might be ill, but I clenched my jaw tight. I refused to spend the next two hours with vomit splattered all over my face and helmet.

The cage slowed. An alto voice cut through my speaker via the long-comm. "Hi, Ana. This is ISRU tech Lily Mason—I work with your mom. I don't know if you remember me, but I'll be the one talking you through this."

"I remember you." Mason was the one who'd thought of using mylar blankets to sew new clothes for growing kids. Mom always said she was both brilliant and easy to talk to—a rare combination. I hoped she could talk me through the mines and safely home again.

"All right, you're stopped. I'm opening the door."

As she said it, the door in front of me fell forward and noiselessly hit the ground.

My headlight illuminated an awkwardly low ceiling. The shaft was supposed to open near a solid wall of rock, but it had to be behind me. A dark, empty expanse stretched before me, only broken by a squat support pillar at the edge of my light.

The place looked like something built by aliens. It certainly hadn't been built for humans. My pulse quickened, pounding against the tightness of my suit.

I took one step out and slipped on the ramp, landing flat on my back. My legs must have fallen asleep or something. I flexed my toes and rubbed my legs as best I could, then scooped up my cleaning kit and the long-comm and stood.

As I began walking, my steps bounced like the ground was rubber. Twice, I hit my head on a low-hanging rock.

"Walk slowly until you're used to it," Mason said. "The spin of the asteroid generates our gravity. You're two and a half kilometers farther inward, so gravity's only ninety percent of what you're used to in there. Keep heading the direction you're going. Do you see a gallery on your right?"

No, I wanted to scream, but I didn't. Just floor and ceiling and darkness ready to swallow me up and crush me under metric tons of unforgiving rock.

I bumped my head again and shrieked.

"Ana?" Mason asked.

I shuffled backward and looked up, ready for giant spiders or evil robots to jump out at me. There was only a low, rough patch on the ceiling.

My hands were clammy, my throat was dry, and I felt like an idiot. "I'm fine."

I kept moving. After a while, my light caught on something up ahead—a wall and a square opening in it. "I see the gallery."

"Good. Keep walking. The equipment's two more kilometers in."

Walking wasn't exactly the right word for my bow-legged gait, but I shuffled along as best I could. The insides of my thighs and lower back already ached from the strain. Two more kilometers. My lungs burned, prickly and tight, but I could make this journey.

The ceiling didn't get any taller when I entered the gallery. At least it was wide—maybe five meters across. My light caught the occasional sparkle of a speck of ice, but it also cast long, flickering shadows over the clawed-out stone. I breathed shallowly and focused on walking. My skin felt cold, shaky, and hot all at once, like I'd come down with a bad fever.

I wished I had Leonhart here to talk to. Or even look at. Something green, something familiar. But he probably wouldn't survive the cold vacuum of space any better than I would, and they didn't make space suits for succulents.

More and more ice glittered on the walls, thickening into a whole vein of it. Soon after that, I reached the end of the gallery and the charge-setter. Just as Mom had said, a capsule of blasting gel had bubbled all over the front of the machine. I prodded the gel with a finger. It had dried all hard and springy, like the rubber turf of the running track in the rec hall.

I pulled out a bottle of solvent, some rags, and a wire brush. I tried to wipe my clammy forehead before I got to work, but of course, my hand just hit the bubble helmet.

When I knelt next to the charge-setter, black spots swarmed my vision. Maybe I really would be ill. I bent down on all fours, trying to catch my breath, but the tightness in my chest didn't fade.

"Ana, your biometrics show you're low on oxygen. Can you check your airpack?"

"Without taking it off?" I tried to look over my shoulder, but it wasn't like the helmet had great mobility.

"Hmm. The long-comm has a camera, but it might be tricky to hold it over your shoulder. If you turn around, we could use the charge-setter's camera to see what's back there."

I did so, one careful step at a time.

Mason swore—a stream of words I knew with at least three I didn't. My stomach lurched, but I swallowed it back down.

"Tell me," I demanded.

"The tube connecting your airpack to the air scrubbers—the stuff that recycles your air so you can breathe for longer—it's been jarred open a crack. Probably when you fell. Reach behind you. Can you grab it?"

My shoulders burned like I was dislocating both of them, but I could only brush the tube with my fingers. I had no leverage to pop it back into place. "N-no."

More swearing.

Cold sweat beaded on my forehead. I licked my dry lips. "Am I going to be okay?"

"You have to come back."

"How much time do I have?" I asked.

"An hour...probably."

I glanced at my wristlet. It had taken me that long to walk here. "*Can* I even make it back?"

She didn't answer. I heard snatches of other voices—none of them Mom or Dad. Did they even know I'd broken my airpack?

I'd tried to save everyone. Instead, I'd just be the first to suffocate.

CHAPTER 6

I bit my lip, thinking. I didn't have enough time to get back, but maybe I had enough time to scrub this machine clean. Maybe I could save Mom, Dad, and Cornelius.

I poured some of the solvent and began scrubbing, blinking away black spots. My head felt huge and airy, my arms detached and heavy. Orange mist rose from the solvent as it began to boil, thanks to the low pressure in the mines. I wiped my brush clean on the rags, then poured more solvent on the machinery.

"Ana." Mason's voice returned. "We want you to stand and start walking back. You're going to make it."

"Not enough good air," I mumbled, my words already sounding slurred in my ears. My hands slipped on the machine's metallic panels. I got one glove smeared in partially dissolved blasting gel. The stuff hardened again, fusing three fingers together.

Mason cleared her throat. "You're...right, unfortunately. Once you get as far as you can, we'll have you vent some heat. We'll keep you cold. Then we'll send someone to bring you back."

I'd heard stories of half-frozen astronauts being brought back to life—you weren't dead until you were warm and dead. But I knew it was a long shot. "None of the techs can fetch me from here."

"We're getting Cornelius suited up as we speak. He's closest, and we don't have any time to waste."

"No!" I scrubbed, the wire brush impossibly heavy in my hand. I wanted to *save* my little brother, not endanger him. "I'll finish it."

My hands doubled in front of me. At this rate, I wouldn't get the charge-setter clean before I passed out.

I leaned my back against the wall, trying to pop the airpack's tube into place. Nothing happened.

I choked back a delirious laugh as I thought about Cornelius finding my corpse. He shouldn't have to come up here, let alone finish the job I'd failed with my body underfoot.

I slumped to the ground next to the charge-setter, leaning heavily on my hand with the blasting gel-fused fingers.

"Ana, you have to start walking. Ana, are you listening?"

I poked the half-solvent goop drooling onto the floor from the charge-setter. Orange mist curled on its surface. "Don't send Cornelius," I mumbled.

Of course they'd send him. Someone had to fix the charge-setter, or everyone in the colony would suffocate. I poked the gel again. It had failed its mission, too. Blasting gel wasn't supposed to ooze everywhere, then harden up.

The fingers I'd been prodding it with dried together, too. Tight.

Airtight?

Wild, frantic hope that tasted like algae, spinach, and hot sauce surged up my throat. With both hands, I scooped as much goopy gel as I could and poured it over my shoulder onto the busted seal of my air scrubber.

The black spots in my vision shrunk, then disappeared. I could feel my toes and fingers properly. A faint, plastic smell circulated into my helmet. As I breathed deeply, the tightness in my chest loosened.

"Ana? Your biometric readings show that your oxygen levels are rising back to normal. That can't—is that right?"

"Don't send Cornelius," I said firmly. Then I carefully poured some solvent on my gloves, picked up the wire brush, and got to work.

THE WALK back through the gallery was no less dark and creepy. The ride down the shaft was just as long and cramped. But my father was waiting for me at the bottom. He fussed over me, practically carrying me into the minecart that took us back to the lab. On the other side of the airlock, I took off my helmet and breathed in clean, abundant air.

Mom and Cornelius were waiting for us. All four of us crushed together in one massive hug that somehow wasn't awkward, even with two airpacks involved.

"The *Platinum Phoenix* might be a dying bird," Mom said, "But thanks to you, it's not dead yet."

I nodded, not wanting to think just yet about how close I'd come to dying myself. I ought to be thrilled, but I was shaky and cold instead.

Thankfully, Cornelius had enough enthusiasm for both of us. "That was awesome! Here!" He whipped around and grabbed something off a counter—he'd brought Leonhart. "I knew you'd come back safe because your plant was waiting for you."

I cupped my succulent in my hands, staring down into that mesmerizing pattern of living green. I loved this little guy, but he wasn't who I'd worried about while I was up in the mines.

I looked up at Cornelius. "Thanks."

"I'm pretty sure no one can fall asleep right now," Cornelius said, "so do you want to crash at home and play *Racing All-Stars Unleashed* with me? I'll let you be first player and pick all the courses."

Our world had nearly ended, but Cornelius was still himself, whole and unharmed. Every centimeter of me ached with exhaustion, but I couldn't stop myself from smiling. "Let's do it."

A WEEK LATER, Governor Cardoso asked to see my parents and me again. The three of us shuffled in. I smiled nervously as I sat. Mom and Dad didn't know what he wanted to talk about, either. Surely, I couldn't be in trouble? But he looked as grave and stern behind his stainless steel desk as he had last time.

"Miss Martins, I'm grateful for your courageous actions. Thank you."

"Umm, you're welcome." I wasn't sure what else to say.

He laced his thin fingers in front of him. "Are you familiar with the Interplanetary Commission, the IC?"

Only vaguely. I nodded, but he seemed to sense my hesitation and explained anyway.

"They're the organization that oversees the Lunar Colonies, our government here, and the Martian colonies—back when those existed. We're required, as part of our charter, to send them daily logs of the happenings on the *Platinum Phoenix*."

And the IC was mad at me for what I'd done? Ecstatic? Governor Cardoso's stern voice revealed nothing.

Dad put his arm around the back of my chair. I could hear his steady breathing and slowed my own to match.

"They briefly considered accusing all adults involved in your mission of child endangerment but eventually decided to declare it an unavoidable emergency."

I swallowed hard. I'd almost gotten my parents and Governor Cardoso *arrested?* How would the IC even try them, with us living all the way out here?

"They've set up regulations and rules should repairs be required in the mines again before we reach Earth and can buy a new fabricator."

My stomach dropped. I'd saved us this time, but we still had eight months before we could make *real* repairs. Something in the mines was bound to break before then.

I'd have to go back to that cold, hard, soundless place.

"And those rules and regulations are?" Dad prompted politely.

"First, that we send a team of three children for safety reasons. If you'd had another person with you, Miss Martins, one of the other children could have remedied the issue with your airpack. With three, if someone is injured, the other two could carry them."

Dread snaked through me as I thought of my classmates. Zoe was just younger and a bit shorter than me. After that, it would be Jayden, the quiet girl who sometimes helped Cornelius and Dae-sung during group work. I didn't want to take either of them up into those low, dark galleries of ice-flecked rock.

"And lastly," Governor Cardoso sighed through his nose, "the colony is to pay you as a contractor for your successful repairs, at a specialist rate the IC has determined fair."

I blinked. My thoughts were still tied up with Zoe and Jayden. "What?"

He tapped his wristlet. "I've transferred the funds. It should be in your parents' accounts now. Good day, Martins."

A PAYCHECK. The idea of *extra* anything felt surreal, let alone extra money. Maybe I could get Zoe a new camera—once we passed Earth, the colony got the parts for the fabricator, and we could buy things like that again.

As my parents and I walked into our apartment, Cornelius paused his video game. "So! Anything exciting?"

"I thought you were finishing your homework while we saw Governor Cardoso," Dad said, but he didn't manage to put any oomph into it.

Cornelius grumbled something under his breath, turned off his game, and headed to his room. Dad turned his calm, gray eyes to me. "If you'd wait in your room a moment, Ana?"

My parents headed to the kitchen to talk. I sat under my loft bed, next to Leonhart. Maybe it was enough money to set up my own mini-aeroponics garden in our living room? Against the wall? We were still eight months away from having a working fabricator again, but the happy possibilities buzzed around my skull.

"Maybe we can get you some friends for keeps," I whispered to Leonhart. "Like some basil. Or mizuna."

It would be fun to grow a little bit of our own food.

Mom and Dad called me back to the living room. They both looked oddly serious—Dad with his hands folded in his lap, Mom with her mouth pursed. I couldn't possibly be in trouble, though.

"Ana," Dad said. "We think you should apply for Mendel Academy."

My heart leaped in my throat, and my face flushed like I'd drunk something hot. "My pay was *that* much? Enough for a ticket to Earth?"

"No, it's about a third. Twenty-thousand ICS."

I exhaled, face cooling, excitement crashing back to reality. Way more than enough to buy Zoe a camera or set up an aeroponics herb garden, but that suddenly seemed small after thinking Earth might be a possibility.

Mom spoke softly. "Your father and I have been saving. Given that most of our salary here comes from profit-sharing... that's been difficult of late. But we can match your paycheck."

I'd had no idea. "Th-thank you," I stammered gratefully.

But it was still only two-thirds of a ticket to Earth.

"If we're lucky, it'll only take one more orbit to save up the rest of it," Dad said. "But it wouldn't hurt to get your application in. Your Grandma Martins would let you stay with her in Porto Alegre."

The possibility made me light-headed. Mendel Academy. Fields of grass. Trees. Open skies.

But I also heard what he didn't say. If something else broke in the next eight months, if I got another paycheck, I could be headed for Earth this orbit. And I ought to prepare for that possibility. I ought to submit my application.

I found myself guiltily hoping that something would break down on the *Platinum Phoenix*.

SEVEN MONTHS LATER

Yet another Tuesday arrived without a mission, a paycheck, or a ticket to Earth. We only had four weeks left until we passed by Earth and could ship in a new fabricator and fix the maintenance robots.

It was better to be alive, I reminded myself, than to have a chance to go to Earth. But thinking that didn't take away the tight longing in my chest.

Since it was Tuesday, I headed down to the ISRU refineries with Zoe, Jayden, Dae-sung, and Cornelius to practice basic repair skills like splicing wires. If anything broke, the *Platinum Phoenix* wanted us to be as prepared as possible. That included having Dae-sung and Cornelius ready to step in if someone else hit a growth spurt or something.

Sometimes Mom supervised, sometimes Lily Mason. But today, curly-haired Daniel Alvez stood at the door to our makeshift workshop. He spoke Portuguese in a quick, Recife accent. As usual, he had a huge grin on his face. Daniel could sound excited about anything. "Well! Here's the whole crew. Ready?"

The room looked the same as it had every week: an empty table in the center and one cart overflowing with random bits of machinery.

"Gloves!" Daniel called.

Zoe rolled her eyes. "We know the drill."

I jammed my fingers into the tight, stretchy fabric. A month until we reached Earth. All this practice would end up being pointless. I'd still be inside the lifeless *Platinum Phoenix* when we left the rest of humanity behind for another two years.

Cornelius tugged at the limp glove. He looked at me with big, sad brown eyes. "I can't get it on. Are you sure it's the right size?"

We did this every Tuesday. It was almost a ritual now. I smiled and responded with the traditional, "That's what the label says."

Daniel laid out piles of bolts, screws, and wires. Jayden and Dae-sung kept up a lively conversation about the soccer World Cup as they practiced using various tools. Our lag time to Earth was down to about two minutes as we got nearer, but that was enough to have them both agonizing over it.

"Can't we practice bare-handed?" Cornelius asked as I walked around the table to him.

"Without a pressure suit, you'd turn to jelly in the mines. So, no. You have to wear them." I stretched the opening of a glove wide enough for him to wrestle it on. Then we got the other one.

Zoe set down her soldering iron. "We do look weird. Like mimes." She pulled a funny face and felt out an invisible wall in front of her.

I picked at my fraying mylar sleeve. "We all look weird *anyway*."

"Point taken."

Daniel tapped his chin with mock-somberness. "If you're worried about looking sharp, you could all do this in full spacesuits. Wanna try?"

Zoe rolled her eyes. "Haha. Very funny. You don't actually want to go through the work of helping us suit up."

"Not really."

Gloves finally on, Cornelius picked up a large socket wrench, one of the easiest tools to use. He struggled to get it over a bolt. Despite all those hours he spent perfecting the lightning-agility of his fingers on video games, he was clumsy in gloves—a disaster waiting to happen.

I practiced with the tiny star-shaped screwdriver. Only Zoe and I were good enough in the gloves to get those finicky screws out with any kind of speed. I'd worked hard to get good at everything—from splicing wires to scrubbing blasting gel. If something else broke down in the mines, those skills could get me away from this metal-plated colony.

I swallowed the creeping feeling in my throat. I shouldn't be *disappointed* we were all safe. Maybe next orbit, or the orbit after, my parents could pay for the rest of my ticket to Earth. Mendel Academy said they'd defer my acceptance until I could get there.

The ISRU refineries didn't make a lot of noise—they operated in a vacuum—but I felt the vibrations through the floor in my bones. I wasn't going to live on this asteroid forever.

I took the star-shaped screw out, then twisted it back in. I never should have applied to Mendel. Having an acceptance letter just made me more disappointed that I couldn't go.

Cornelius held his socket wrench with two hands and squinted at the chunky bolt like it would try to run away. He hadn't gotten it halfway tightened yet. "So," he said to me, "we're about a month away from Earth."

Great. The exact topic I didn't want to talk about. "Yeah, we're close."

"Then there probably won't be another mission, right? You're not going to Earth?"

He might as well have punched me in the diaphragm.

"Because it's really, really unlikely now that anything will break before we can get a new fabricator. You'll stay on the *Platinum Phoenix*, right?" Cornelius asked hopefully.

I lost focus and snapped my thin, brittle screw in two. Now I'd need a drill to get it out. "Thanks for reminding me."

He fiddled with his socket wrench. "Things will be better once everything's repaired."

"Better? We'll still live in stainless steel rooms breathing recycled air. Even if we get a hundred research grants, the *Platinum Phoenix* will always be the *Platinum Phoenix*."

Cornelius chewed on his lip. "When everything's fixed, I'm going to eat a hundred strawberries."

All the asteroid kids played this game. I was supposed to outdo him by bragging I'd eat a thousand cherry tomatoes or a mountain of lettuce. Cornelius was trying to cheer me up, but right then, it wasn't enough.

"Isn't there a new DLC for *The Sky is Rising?*" I asked.

Cornelius beamed and began talking as rapidly as Daniel did. He gestured with both gloved hands, socket wrench forgotten. He drew Dae-sung and Jayden into the conversation. They all played games together. Given our lag time, it was impossible to play with anyone from Earth.

That left Zoe and me to talk about whatever, but my heart wasn't in it. Would I feel better once we'd passed Earth? Or would that make everything more depressing?

At least Cornelius was happy here. I wished I could feel the same way.

As the oldest kids, Daniel asked Zoe and me to stay behind and clean up. He helped, too, until his teenage son, Lucas, popped in. They stepped outside to chat, leaving the two of us to finish ourselves.

"Cornelius doesn't get it, does he?" Zoe asked. She dumped a handful of bolts into a tray, letting them all clatter against each other.

I laid wrenches, screwdrivers, and soldering irons back in their place. "How to do repairs or the part where I want to leave?"

"Well, both. But I didn't mean repairs. So close to Earth, and no mission in sight. You miserable?"

I tried to laugh at myself and failed. Why did everyone have to keep bringing it up? "You're good at reading faces."

"Nah." Zoe used her thumbs and index finger to make a box, framing me like she was about to take a picture. "Your face is saying a lot more than a thousand words. All of them a variety of *I want to get to Earth.* I don't blame you."

"Thanks. You want to leave, too?"

"Who wouldn't? Except for Cornelius, of course. I think your little brother's got a few bolts loose upstairs."

I scowled. I might make fun of Cornelius sometimes, but I hated it when other people did.

Zoe started wrapping up the wires. "Oh, don't get all defensive. It's true. At least the adults chose to come here, but all of us born on the asteroid...we deserve a chance to get off."

"A chance we'll never get," I grumbled, grabbing another fistful of wires.

Zoe pursed her lips, then whispered, "Do you feel cheated? You almost died up there, and after everything you went through...it's not even going to get you out of here."

That cold memory returned. The way my lungs squeezed and my vision fuzzed, all alone with nothing but kilometers and kilometers of heavy, red rock around me. "That's not why I went up."

We were alive. That's what mattered. The fact that Mendel was painfully close to a possibility... I needed to forget that. I needed to be able to lay on my bed and daydream about the academy instead of ache for it.

"Yeah," Zoe said. "That doesn't mean you can't feel like crap about being stuck."

I nodded, throat tight. She was right about that.

Zoe waved for me to help her move the tables back against the wall. The feet screeched against the metallic floor. Then we headed out, waving to Daniel and Lucas as we passed. Our mylar slippers made soft slapping noises on the metal floor of the empty hallways.

"I didn't mention this before, but since I'm not leaving...I wanted to get you a better camera. I've seen you looking at the Z-Scope 42."

She peered at me, face serious. "You'd do that?"

"It's not *that* expensive." I was pretty sure it would be around 300 ICS. I'd have to pay the colony for materials and time with the fabricator, then pay Z-Scope for one-time-use plans. If I wasn't making it to Earth this time around, I could at least do something nice for Zoe.

She scuffed her feet on the floor instead of gushing with delight like I'd imagined. "You risk your life, and you get a *camera?* It's not even for you!"

"I didn't mean to make you upset," I mumbled. What was wrong with her?

Zoe put her hand on my shoulder. "Sorry. Sorry. You're being super-nice. I was just thinking about something else. You actually helped me make up my mind about it."

"What?"

"Just something I've been thinking about. Don't worry about the camera. I've earned enough from my photos to buy a new one, once there's a fab again."

"Oh, do you think...you'll ever have enough to get to Earth?"

She laughed, a dry, bitter sound. "I'd be stuck photographing this asteroid until I'm two hundred. You're a *lot* closer to buying a ticket than me."

Close, but not close enough.

Two DAYS LATER, I sat at the cramped aluminum table in my family's apartment, slurping down my breakfast ration—a foil packet of algae—while I helped Cornelius finish his homework. "Line up the decimal first, then subtract."

"Thanks." He scribbled furiously on the notebook-sized piece of glass he'd attached his bar-comp to. "You're the best."

Helping him was kind of fun—and I needed something other than the flavor of breakfast to think about. "So last night when you told Dad you were staying up late to finish your math..."

"I *meant* to, but I needed to save my game first. And I got a little distracted. I did explain how cool the new DLC is for *The Sky is Rising*, right?" He paused, tapping his stylus against the glass. "So, with this problem, umm..."

"The answer's fifty-six." I shook my head. "You know you're a terrible procrastinator, right?"

He beamed at me. "Sure. But it always works out because you're here."

As always, Cornelius looked happy as he rushed through his last-minute work.

My wristlet buzzed. I set down my food and tapped the wristlet's face.

"What is it?" Cornelius leaned closer to see, knocking over his barely-touched algae foil. Dark-green goo dribbled onto the aluminum table. He mumbled at the mess and fetched a rag.

The tiny projector on the side of my wristlet spilled the message in blue light over my mylar sleeve. "Ana Alessandra

Pereira Martins. Report to decompression suit-up this evening at 1900 hours. The shifter has broken and requires maintenance. We've also notified your parents and sent messages to Zoe Palmer and Jayden Jones, who you will be leading through this mission."

I stared at it, perfectly still as my pulse raced. Nervous excitement buzzed through my bones. Nerves and algae tasted gross together, but I didn't mind.

I had a mission.

CHAPTER 8

I couldn't stop my stomach from tightening as I remembered the mines' darkness and creepy low ceilings. But when I finished this job, I'd get a paycheck. In four short weeks, I could leave this asteroid forever and head to Earth.

Cornelius looked over my shoulder. "What is it?"

I tapped the message off. No need to freak him out. "Nothing. Just some, um, school stuff."

"You wouldn't hide school stuff." He slumped back in his chair, then wiped up his spilled algae.

I innocently sipped my electrolyte water. "I don't want you to tease me about how behind I am on my paper."

Cornelius frowned at me.

"Fine. I don't want you to feel bad about how awesome it is."

"It's a mission, isn't it?" he demanded.

Even though he said *mission* like a dirty word, it sent a thrill up my spine.

"You won't really go to Earth, will you?" he asked. The recycler vent whined in the ceiling, sucking up dust and loose skin cells.

"Why would I stay here if I didn't have to?"

Cornelius' lip quivered as he glared at me. "You're an ugly bucket of dross!"

I flinched. If he couldn't be happy for me, he could at least leave me alone. "You're just jealous, Corny!"

"Don't call me that!"

We should be celebrating together. Why couldn't he be happy for me? "Corny, Corny, Corny!"

He ran down the hall and slammed his door. I wished I had something to slam back at him. He shouldn't be mad about staying behind! It wasn't like I could buy tickets for both of us. A lifetime of studying plants awaited me. Cornelius, though? His interest in Earth seemed to start and end with game release dates. He'd never acted interested in leaving the *Platinum Phoenix.*

I finished my foil, then dumped mine and Cornelius' into the recycler chute in the wall. A nagging voice in the back of my head—it sounded a lot like Dad—said I should talk to Cornelius. Ask him why he was so upset.

But if I tried to talk to Cornelius while he finished getting ready for school, I'd just gloat. Or yell at him again.

There'd be plenty of time to talk to Cornelius tomorrow, after the mission. I slipped into my room.

"We're making it, Leonhart." I gave one of his leaves a tiny high-five, but it was kind of pathetic. I sighed. I'd get a real high-five from Zoe when school started.

I turned my wristlet to project on the silvery wall and tapped up the main page for Mendel Academy. I always kept it up and refreshed on my bar-comp, so I didn't have to wait through the lag time to Earth.

The familiar purple and gold page banner sparkled across the table: *Academia Mendel, est.* 2042. The photos showed students collecting flora samples out in the Pampas or smiling in their classrooms. They wore neat-pressed slacks, skirts, and blazers—no mylar clothes for them.

I ran my fingers over the photos of those happy students, distorting the pictures. Did they all love botany as much as me? Did they realize how lucky they were to see so many plants every day?

I gazed at all the pictures, even though I'd seen them before. Students peered down microscopes in labs, wrote on bar-comps out on the endless grass of the Pampas, or lounged about the green, shrub-filled campus. I tapped up the recruitment vids and mouthed along. I'd memorized the words months ago.

When those finished, I glanced around. "Cornelius?"

He should have been ready for school by now.

"Cornelius?" I left the kitchen and opened his bedroom door. Empty. He'd walked to class without me.

Dread prickled up my chest. "Wristlet. Time."

A number projected over my mylar sleeve. 0932 hours.

I was late for school.

I TRIED to slip in unnoticed, but I wasn't halfway to Zoe's table when Dad's calm, stern voice cut across the room. "Ana Alessandra Pereira Martins."

I froze. Some of the kids giggled. Zoe hadn't even noticed— she had her earbuds in and was resting her head on her hands like she was about to nod off. Cornelius glared at me, his eyes red from crying. I wanted to snap at him for ditching me.

"In my office." Dad gestured for me to go first.

I shuffled into the small side room with huge windows. Everyone could still see us, but no one could hear us.

I plopped down on one of the two aluminum chairs. They matched the wall paneling. Aluminum didn't sell for much on Earth or the moon, so we used it—or other cheap metals like steel—for everything. Whoever designed these chairs made them look round and comfortable, but appearances weren't everything. I squirmed as soon as I sat.

"I got the message about your mission tonight." As always,

Dad kept his tone even. That only made me feel like I was in more trouble. "You're excited, aren't you?"

"Of course I am!"

Dad shook his head. "You shouldn't be."

"I thought you and Mom wanted me to go to Earth. I thought you'd been saving up for it." I glanced out the glass window. Some forty heads whipped back around to their work. My face burned. "You got to live in space and on Earth. Why is it wrong that I want to do the same?"

"It isn't wrong. But that doesn't mean I want to send my daughter deep into the asteroid, *again*, where the carved-out galleries hold nothing but dangerous machinery and hard vacuum."

Memories of the silent darkness crept across my skin, giving me chills.

"You've...you've been brave," Dad fumbled. His mouth pursed into his most-serious thinking expression. "You kept everyone alive."

I could hear the *but* coming.

"And I'm proud that you're dedicated to continuing your education."

I knew he meant it, and he was trying to put me at ease. But the compliments only made my stomach writhe as I waited for the scolding to follow.

"I *am* disappointed, however, that you are late."

At last: the lecture. "It's not my fault! Cornelius—"

"We're not talking about Cornelius. I get that you're excited about the future. But right now, it's making you *careless*. You can't be careless in the mines."

"I know!" I knew it better than he did. He hadn't been up there, alone, breathing unscrubbed air.

"Furthermore..." he cleared his throat, and something guilty crept into his eyes. "I'm not sure this mission is necessary."

"Necessary? Has Mom miraculously fixed the fab or the robots?"

"No." Dad leaned back in his chair. "But we're only four weeks from Earth. With that great ice vein we hit last month, we'll make it to Earth without any further mining."

"By how much?" I demanded.

Dad reddened. "A day after the scheduled fab delivery."

"You expect the techs to install a new fab, have it running, repair the maintenance robots, fix the shifter, and start mining again *in a day?*"

"We could also buy extra water rations from the Lunar Colonies to tide us over," Dad said.

"A month without mining? Even if we could do without the ice, the *Platinum Phoenix* needs every bit of profit it can get to buy more supplies." The cost of a new fab—10 million ICS—made my twenty grand paycheck look like spare change.

"I'm worried that's what Governor Cardoso and CEO Yun think, and that's the real reason they're sending you up into the mines. I've filed a formal complaint. The IC has already ruled to leave the decision up to the colony. There will be an open-attendance hearing at 1630 hours to hear the opinions of colony employees. Then the governing board of the *Platinum Phoenix* will make a final decision."

"Dad!" I *needed* that paycheck. He couldn't ask the board to strip that away—to keep me here.

"Ana, we live on an asteroid. I know that's easy to forget."

Forget? When everything was made of glass and aluminum?

"Thanks to the asteroid's spin, we live at a comfortable gravity," Dad continued. "We have wide halls and nice chairs. Friends and family. But this is still an asteroid."

Judging by the dramatic pause, he'd nearly reached the thesis of his lecture. "Doesn't it unsettle you? The techs have been so careful. They thought we wouldn't have any more problems, and now this."

"Stuff breaks," I mumbled. "It's all old."

"Old and unpredictable. Your mother told me they had a massive computer meltdown near ore-intake at the ISRU refineries last night. They lost all their data. What else is crumbling? What if the cage cables snap?"

If it happened while I was in the cage, I wouldn't have much time to think about it. If it happened while I was in the mines, I'd be trapped. I wouldn't starve to death because I'd run out of oxygen first.

"Space is not forgiving of overconfidence," Dad said.

I shifted on my hard aluminum chair. He was being paranoid. Overprotective. "If the board decides to send me, will you refuse to sign the consent papers?"

Dad exhaled slowly. "If they deem it necessary for our survival, maybe *I'm* being overconfident that our air and water won't run out. Yes, I'll sign the release. But," he laid both of his hands on my shoulders, voice hoarse, "*if* you go, I want you to be careful. I want you to remember where we live and how dangerous that is."

"Of course I'll be careful!" That too-tight feeling crept up my throat again. "Stop trying to scare me!"

I stormed out of the office, even though all the other kids were watching. How could he try to toss away my future without even asking me?

I dropped into the chair next to Zoe. My lungs prickled, and my hands trembled. I sucked in the abundant, recycled air. She yawned and popped out her earbuds. "You grounded?"

"No."

"Good." She rubbed her eyes. She must have stayed up late editing photos again. "Excited for our mission tonight?"

Excited wasn't the right word. Especially after seeing that one of my crew members was half-asleep. "You should get excused from IDPOP and take a nap this afternoon."

"I was planning on napping through class this morning...but that's probably a better plan. My bed is way comfier than this."

I glanced around the room to check on Jayden. Her teeth chattered, and her legs were bouncing.

"Hey, Jayden," I whispered.

She jumped, then turned toward me. "Y-yes?"

"You all right?"

"Of...of course," she stuttered.

Great. One sleepy crewmate and one who looked ready to shriek at the drop of a pin. Dad wanted me to be appropriately fearful and cautious, but nervous jitters might be just as dangerous as overconfidence.

I slouched in my chair and pretended to read my assignment. Zoe and Jayden had months of training, and they had another kid—me—who'd been in the mines before. But they still weren't ready. Even if it wasn't as safe, part of me wished the IC would send me alone.

Maybe crawling into asteroid mines wasn't the kind of thing anyone could be ready for. I'd have to be a solid leader tonight— both alert and calm while I led my team through the repairs.

That is, if we got to go at all.

CHAPTER 9

As soon as school opened to project work, Dae-sung gave me a solid hi-five. "Congrats!"

"Thanks!" It was easier to act cheerful than to explain how the board might cancel the mission.

"You're really going to make it to Earth, huh? You've got to eat a mountain of stuff for us. What are you going to try first?"

Oh, oh the possibilities. "I'm going to gorge myself at a churrascaria." Mom talked about them with such nostalgia, their food had to be delicious. I especially wanted to try the roasted pineapple. I'd never eaten pineapple before—let alone pineapple cooked over open flames.

Cornelius stuck his tongue out at me. I ignored him.

"I hope it's fantastic, Ana. You'll have to write me because I'm staying put," Dae-sung said proudly.

"Oh?"

"Yeah. Do you know how many crazy awesome things I'm going to make up here? The zero-g rec hall is just the *beginning.*"

I grinned, the tension easing from my shoulders. Dae-sung made it sound like the mission was already over and all I had to do was wait for my shuttle. He had a knack for putting people at ease, and right now, I was grateful for it.

Zoe stifled a yawn. "Congrats." Her voice was flat. "Do you want to hold my reflectors again?"

She looked worse than Mom after a double shift. "Sorry, I've actually got something else to work on today. Maybe you should ask my Dad to let you go home now? Rest up and all?"

Zoe shrugged and shuffled off. I dug into creating a report for my dad, filling it with everything I'd learned about being safe in the mines—from space suit readiness to first aid. I even read all about the shifter I'd be repairing. The machine did what its name implied—moved blasted rubble around the mines. Before I left on this mission, I'd prove to Dad that I wasn't being reckless. I was prepared.

Zoe got excused to sleep, so I headed to IDPOP in aeroponics alone. She needed the rest, but I still wished she had the chance to photograph something green, something different. She loved aeroponics every bit as much as I did.

As soon as I stepped into the humid, living air of aeroponics, I breathed easier. Dr. Fletcher was working on one of the huge glass screens near the door. I could see Dr. Kim, too, back in the shelves of plants, but she didn't look up. She opened a drawer lined with a special mesh. Hundreds of wire-thin stems with tiny cotyledon leaves grew above it. Below hung the plants' hairy white roots, still glittering with a recent spray of nutrients.

"Ah! It's good to see you, Ana." Dr. Fletcher stood, redid her messy bun, then shook my hand. "Ready for an interesting project?"

"Always!"

"Good. Someone around here ought to do something exciting today, and it isn't me. I've been working on grant writing." She wrinkled her nose. "Grant writing is the most boring kind of writing in the world."

"I bet," I agreed with a sympathetic eye roll.

"Pull up a seat." She gestured to the chair next to hers and flicked some spreadsheets from her glass screen over to the one in front of me. "I've grabbed the most recent data from our crop of peas—the ones we grow short-term for shoots, not the crop for seeds. And here's the data from all past crops. I want you to compare these."

Dr. Fletcher gave me real work. I adored her for that.

I bit my lip as an idea nibbled at my brain. Dr. Fletcher had written my recommendation letter to Mendel Academy. She cared about me getting into that school. The board wouldn't listen to me, but they might listen to her if she didn't outright scold me as Dad had.

I glanced at my wristlet. 1330. The hearing started in three hours. What could Dr. Fletcher do in so little time? She was already back at her computer, scowling at her grant.

On any other day, I would have torn into the data. I started reluctantly, my stomach waffling with uncertainty. Should I ask her for help? I couldn't find the words, so I sorted the data instead. When I finished, I hesitantly cleared my throat.

Dr. Fletcher swiveled her chair toward me. "Well?"

"The peas aren't growing as well as they did last orbit."

Dr. Fletcher nodded. "Are they the same, or different, from the generations since the fab broke?"

Using the small control screen on the desk in front of me, I filtered out any data older than thirteen months, then studied what was still left on the large glass. "This is the worst one yet as we're conserving more and more water, but it's pretty close to the other ones, except for this aisle of trays. They're all much slower-growing."

"That's about what I expected." Dr. Fletcher leaned back in her chair. "Do you know why that quarter is slower?"

I moved my fingers in the air in front of the glass, pulling charts to this side or that. It took a minute, but Dr. Fletcher waited for me.

"The slow ones were seeded more closely together than normal," I answered.

"Exactly right. We decided to experiment with denser

plantings. We used the same amount of nutrient solution in the auto-sprayers. Eventually, the dense trays do produce pea shoots." She pulled up their profile on the glass. "Per edible ounce, though, which plant spacing uses less water?"

"I'll...need a bit of time to figure that out."

Dr. Fletcher smiled warmly, the corners of her eyes crinkling. "Well, get at it then."

If I didn't ask now, it would be too late. My mouth felt as dry as if the ISRU refineries had sucked all the hydrogen and oxygen out of me. "Dr. Fletcher? I'm...I'm worried about the hearing. Can you do anything to stop them from canceling the mission? I want to make it to Mendel."

The color seeped out of her face. Her mouth turned into a flat line.

I winced and pulled back. She was going to lecture me, just like Dad.

"*What* hearing?"

I blinked. "All the *Platinum Phoenix* employees were invited. Didn't you get a memo?"

Dr. Fletcher scowled and tapped her wristlet. Only as she scanned messages did I notice the haggard bags under her eyes —ones not unlike my mom's. Being in charge of everyone's food during a drought was probably just as stressful as trying to keep the mines running.

"Sure enough," she muttered. "A hearing."

My heart pounded as I waited for what she'd say next.

She looked up at me, her voice diamond-hard. "I'll do whatever I can for you. You don't deserve to be trapped on this doomed rock."

I'd never seen her like this—all of her warmth gone. I peered at her. "You want to go back to Earth too, don't you?"

"Any reasonable person would. But at least I chose to come here in the first place. You didn't. I can't believe someone's trying to yank away your chance to escape." Her mouth tightened. "You deserve a lifeboat out of here."

"Lifeboat?" The word sounded vaguely familiar—maybe from some old vid?

"Escape pod, then."

I frowned. Technicians had stripped the *Platinum Phoenix*'s escape pods for their air recyclers and other parts over a year ago. The pods weren't capable of landing on the Moon or Earth anyway. One of those wouldn't get me anywhere.

Dr. Fletcher sighed. "Never mind. I'll do everything I can."

She swept out of the room. I stared after for a long minute. I didn't know she cared about my education that much. Dad loved me and always would, but Dr. Fletcher understood what I loved.

I'D JUST FINISHED my calculations—the closely spaced, slower-growing plants used less water per edible ounce—when Dr. Kim strolled up behind me.

"Where did Dr. Fletcher go?" Dr. Kim asked in Portuguese, with only a slight accent marking her as a non-native speaker.

I couldn't tell if she was curious or upset or something else; she spoke in the same flat tone she always used. Nervously rubbing the back of my neck, I explained about the hearing. Dr. Kim didn't look at me, though, or show any sign of listening. Her sharp eyes scoured my work. "You forgot to calculate for evaporation and the current efficiency of the water recyclers."

My heart sank.

She sat next to me, tucking her black hair—cut in a no-nonsense bob—behind her ears. She pulled up a few more charts. "Here. Recalculate using these."

She turned back to her work. I wiped my hands on my

mylar pants and glanced over my shoulder. Dr. Kim wasn't monitoring me; she was already engrossed in something on her bar comp. She trusted me to do this.

Either that, or she didn't care what I did and didn't want to waste any more time talking to me. Zoe thought the way Dr. Kim hyperfocused on her research and tuned everything else out was creepy; she could go entire IDPOPs without noticing that students were in aeroponics with her and Dr. Fletcher. It often took extra effort to get her attention. Dad had told me that kind of zeroed-in concentration wasn't uncommon among autistic people.

Even though I found her intimidating, I couldn't help but admire Dr. Kim's dedication. Did she work so hard because she loved it here, or did she secretly miss Earth, like Dr. Fletcher?

Did my parents feel like Dr. Fletcher? I'd never asked. Part of me didn't want to. Plenty of the adults still whole-heartedly believed in the *Platinum Phoenix*. Escaping to Earth would be bittersweet if I knew that my family would never follow, even if they saved enough money to buy shuttle tickets for everyone.

I swallowed all my worries and focused on the numbers, trying to be as meticulous and careful as Dr. Kim.

I resolved the problem. The regularly spaced crop was more efficient, after all.

I STAYED IN AEROPONICS, working on my self-assigned report for Dad until Dr. Kim told me she was locking up. Dr. Fletcher never came back.

"May I walk with you to the vote?" Dr. Kim asked.

"Vote?"

"I suppose they didn't send the message to the children. The board decided to settle the matter of the mission by employee vote."

I followed her out of aeroponics. "Does that make it more or less likely for the mission to happen?"

"The board needs a supermajority in cases involving minors. Popular vote only requires a simple majority."

I squinted at her. Aeroponics and the mines—those I understood. Asteroid politics were a lot less clear.

Dr. Kim sighed. "Yes, it's more likely for the mission to continue."

Had Dr. Fletcher made this change happen?

We strolled by several doors in the hallway, all stamped with *PP* encircled by the wings of an ancient phoenix. Dr. Kim clasped her hands behind her back. "I hear you want to be a botanist."

"Yes, Dr. Kim." I couldn't tell if she was about to lecture me or not.

"I had to beat out a thousand other candidates for my position here, back when things were good. Many of them were better scientists than me, but they lacked the language skills or some other qualification. Now I'm doing experiments no one else can."

I frowned.

"You, though. You're already here. No job application required." She gave me a smile so subtle I might have been imagining it.

"I want to study more than just trays."

Dr. Kim nodded. "You've heard about the droughts in Kansas, USA?"

"No." I read about Earth plants all the time, but I rarely looked at current events.

"Aeroponics is very water-efficient. More than soil-planted crops, more than hydroponics. Our data here is helping them create low-water solutions to feed starving people. Our work is important. You could be a part of it. Thousands of scientists on Earth can survey forests or examine mushrooms under microscopes. But there are few botanists here."

"Thank you," I said politely. I loved aeroponics, but Mendel Academy and the lushness of the Pampas were waiting for me. I wanted *fields*, even if I was one in a thousand studying the grass.

Dr. Fletcher understood that.

We entered the high-ceilinged recreation hall. The track and tennis courts stood empty, and chairs covered the soccer field's dull green synthetic turf. At the front, the governing board sat near the podium, facing the audience.

"I see your dad," Dr. Kim said, pointing toward him in the middle-back of the seats. "You should join your family. The hearing's about to start."

CHAPTER 10

I squeezed through the row to sit by Dad. He put an arm around my shoulder, fingers too tight. Protective. Cornelius sat on the other side of him with his feet dangling and his head down.

"How was aeroponics?" Dad asked.

"Good." I'd worked on a cool problem, and I'd nearly finished my report for him. I thought about showing it to him, but the hall was so loud and crowded, I didn't think he could appreciate it right now.

I'd share it before I left on the mission. *If* I left. Surely everyone would vote for the mission to go forward, wouldn't they?

I glanced at Cornelius. He wasn't even playing a video game on his wristlet, just staring at the floor. "What's up with him?"

My brother flinched away from me.

"Be nice, Ana," Dad chided.

I wasn't trying to tease him. But saying as much wouldn't help. "Where's Mom?"

"Here!" she huffed, climbing over our neighbors. I slid down a chair so she could sit next to Dad. Her shirt was crinkled, and those exhausted wrinkles lined her eyes. She gave Dad a tired kiss on the cheek, then asked Cornelius and me about school—as if this were just any other day. She didn't mention the mission. Maybe she didn't want to think about it.

The chairs around us swelled with people. Within a few

minutes, the crowd grew to at least three hundred—about half the asteroid's population. Apparently, people had an opinion about this mission.

The adults wore their uniforms or lab coats—patched with bits of mylar. I'd never heard an adult complain about it. As Dr. Fletcher had pointed out, they all *chose* to come. Would they understand why I wanted to leave?

Governor Cardoso stood, and the rec hall fell silent.

According to procedure, Governor Cardoso checked his wristlet to determine the language the gathered attendees had the greatest proficiency in, then spoke in Korean. Mom popped her earbuds in for the Portuguese translation. Just to make sure I didn't miss anything, I followed suit. My Korean vocabulary leaned heavily toward school subjects and soccer. I usually heard asteroid politics and news about the mines at home.

Governor Cardoso described our current water and air supplies. If we left the shifter to sit useless in the mines, we were gambling that nothing else would break before we reached Earth. He then gave a long list of things that had broken and couldn't be repaired since the fab went down, including the maintenance robots.

My heart pounded in my throat. He was arguing *for* the mission.

He finished by praising my bravery on the last mission and saying how he knew Zoe and Jayden also had the courage to save this asteroid.

CEO Yun stood next. She had the same steely hair as Governor Cardoso, and the same resolve in her words—all in support of the mission. When she finished, she opened the floor for comments.

Navigator Stewart jumped to his feet first. "Planning on nothing going wrong on this asteroid is suicidal. That's all we need to know."

Nurse Oliveira stood next, glaring at Stewart. I was used to hearing her speak Portuguese with a soft Bahian accent, but she kept it in Korean and curtly spat out the syllables. "Everyone here is practically a cannibal if we're going to throw children up into those mines when the need isn't dire. I can't believe—"

"By the time the need's dire, it might be too late to save anyone!" Nurse Hwang interjected. "That *includes* the children!"

The two nurses kept arguing, shouting over each other. The translator couldn't keep up. Eventually, CEO Yun intervened and made them both sit down.

Surprisingly, Dr. Kim stood next. She folded her hands in front of her as though she were examining charts on the glass in her lab. It took me a moment to realize the translator had switched to Korean.

I popped my earbuds out. Despite being natively fluent in Korean, Dr. Kim had rudely switched to Portuguese. It felt like she wanted me to hear first-hand what she had to say, though she stared ahead at the board.

"The Interplanetary Commission is watching us. I believe they're letting us vote because they don't want to be responsible for sending children into the mines. If something goes wrong again—like that broken seal on Ana's air scrubber—they can hold us accountable. It will have been our choice after all. They could cite the colony with negligence and open child protection cases for all minors here.

"I don't want to see this colony's children taken away to Earth for a lengthy investigation. I believe that for the *Platinum Phoenix* to succeed, we need these children to step up into the roles we have carved out onto this asteroid. We have precious few children here. Let's not squander them and their potential to build up this remarkable asteroid with our greed for a month's worth of heavy metals to sell."

She sat just as smoothly as she'd stood.

I turned to Dad, frowning. "Could the IC do that? Take all the kids away?"

"There'd have to be a lot of political pressure from Earth," he mumbled, shaking his head. "That many tickets to Earth would eat up a huge chunk of the IC's budget."

I bit my lip. If the IC opened a case, I wouldn't have to pay for my ticket to Earth. I'd still have my savings—a small fortune—left over.

But my parents weren't criminals. I didn't want to see them accused. And however much I wanted to leave the *Platinum Phoenix*, I didn't want my home torn apart by the IC. If their political bickering could kill a half-built space elevator, I didn't want to imagine what they might do to us.

I spotted Dr. Fletcher's messy blonde bun in the front row, but she didn't stand. I wished I could speak for myself, tell everyone about Mendel Academy, but I wasn't an employee. I wasn't allowed to comment.

After another dozen speakers, Governor Cardoso rose. "All employees, please vote now on your wristlets."

My stomach churned. I wasn't supposed to, but I watched both my parents tap their wristlets. Negative. Against. They still didn't want to send me.

I shifted on my hard, aluminum chair. Dr. Fletcher would vote yes. Dr. Kim, no. The nurses who'd spoken canceled each other out. What about everyone else?

Heads bobbed back up as people finished voting. Governor Cardoso checked the results on his wristlet. "We have five hundred and twelve votes in, both from employees present and employees voting from their workstations, with fifty-one abstaining." He cleared his throat. I stopped breathing. "The mission will continue tonight, as planned. Thank you for your participation."

I exhaled, a rush of giddy relief filling me. Tonight! 1900 hours. I checked my wristlet; I had an hour and a half until then. I'd go through the mines once more, and then I'd be done with all of this.

A horrible retching noise cut through the air, and the crowd near the front sprang back. Nurse Hwang and Nurse Oliveira both ran forward. They put their arms around someone and started leading her out. Jayden. She was shaking even worse than she had been during school. She threw up again, all over the artificial grass.

Nerves, or had she come down with something?

"Well." Governor Cardoso frowned. "Apparently, it won't be Ana, Zoe, and Jayden this time. Let me check who's next on the list." Governor Cardoso turned to his wristlet.

I searched the crowd for Dae-sung. Poor guy—assigned a mission last-minute. It wasn't like he needed the money for a ticket to Earth. Zoe and I would probably do the actual repair work since we were faster. But I wouldn't mind having Dae-sung's level-headed optimism with us when we stared down the darkness of the mines tonight. But before I could spot him, Cornelius stood. Loudly, he announced, "I volunteer."

 CHAPTER 11

The inside of my mouth turned to talc. Was Cornelius making fun of me? Was he that jealous? Or was he too dumb to realize this was dangerous?

I wondered if that's how Dad felt about me going.

Dad jumped to his feet faster than Mom. "You can't send both my children up that mining shaft!"

"You'd rather force one of your other students than allow your son to go?" Governor Cardoso retorted.

Dad stilled.

Far to the right of us, Dae-sung started to stand, but Cornelius waved him down. Dae-sung frowned, but he sat.

My brother spoke. "If this is worth risking Ana's life, then it's worth risking mine, too."

Mom stirred, her groggy head finally processing the situation. "Cornelius...why?"

"I want to." His hands twitched at his sides, almost making fists.

The lines around Dad's mouth made him look a decade older. "I propose we retake the vote now that we know who's going."

"The results are final," Governor Cardoso said. "As Cornelius' guardian, you can refuse to send him. You could keep Ana here too—the only experienced child and the intended leader of this small group. We'd just have to find others to replace them."

From his confident tone, Governor Cardoso already knew Dad and Mom wouldn't push this responsibility onto his younger, untrained students.

I imagined Cornelius' round face inside a helmet. He knew how horrible he was at doing anything with gloves on. And going on the mission wouldn't get him to Earth. It wouldn't get him anything.

Why had he volunteered? I'd worked so hard last time to keep him out of the mines! I'd scrubbed up blasting gel even as I suffocated. When I thought I'd die anyway, I gave my all to keep Cornelius safe at home. All my muscles tightened, remembering those moments.

I'd never told him about it. But volunteering—it was like he'd spat in my face. I ground my teeth together so I wouldn't shout at him, right there in front of everyone.

Mom reached for Dad's hand. They shared a look—a wordless conversation I couldn't follow. Dad's shoulders dropped.

Mom turned to Governor Cardoso. "Cornelius will go."

Despite the clamor around us, we headed home in stiff, tense silence. My parents looked at us with pain-pinched eyes. I glared at Cornelius. Stupid, stupid Cornelius. As we walked, fear spiked in my gut. Could I keep him safe in the mines?

We picked up dinner from food processing, then sat around our kitchen table. I peeled my foil back—lentil cakes and nutritional yeast. At least there wasn't any algae sauce.

I ate because I was hungry and because not eating wouldn't help anything. I was halfway done when Dad's voice cut across the quiet. "Ana, take care of your brother tonight."

He shouldn't be coming at all. "Why not just send me and Zoe if he's such a baby?"

Cornelius glowered.

"Ana, watch your mouth," Mom said.

"I'm being honest! He's horrible at repairs—the worst in the group by far."

Cornelius tightened his grip on his fork. "I want to go with you while I can, all right? I don't have to be good at repairs. You and Zoe can do that. I'll only be there in case someone gets injured. That's why the IC said there has to be three of us, right?"

"If anyone gets injured up there, it'll be you," I snapped. "You can't even put on your own gloves, Corny."

"Don't call me that!"

"*Children!*" Mom yelled.

That shut both of us up.

But I was right. Dad worried that I'd act recklessly, but Cornelius had beaten me to it.

"I've got some homework to do before the mission," Cornelius mumbled. He slunk away, taking his dinner with him. Usually, there was a strict food-at-the-table rule, but neither Mom nor Dad stopped him.

I looked down at my food and scooped up another piece of lentil cake. Thoughts of what could go wrong gnawed on me. Since Cornelius was only coming to spite me, wouldn't that make it my fault if something went wrong? He shouldn't be on this mission.

Mom set down her fork and went to talk to Cornelius. I sat alone with Dad around a table that, for the first time in months, had uneaten food abandoned on it.

"Ana," Dad said, "don't tease him. At least until you're both back unharmed. Squabbling during the mission will only make it more dangerous."

"I wasn't teasing! He'll be useless on this mission. It's not safe for him."

"It's not safe for anyone. Should I keep you here? Make one of your classmates go instead?" he asked.

I swigged down some water, then projected my report onto the table—all the safety stuff, first aid, and repair procedures I'd written up. "I wish I'd had more time to work on this, but look. I know how to navigate the mines."

Unlike Cornelius—he only knew how to navigate his video games.

"Yes, Ana. You're smart." He barely glanced at the report I'd made just for him. "But space isn't a test. Being smart won't save you if the mines collapse. Or keep you warm if your suit fails. The universe is a vast, dangerous place that we are just a tiny part of. Even our best scientists understand only a little of how it works, and we control it even less."

I glared at him. I'd done extra homework on my own, and he was still lecturing me.

"You shouldn't be excited that the hearing allowed this mission," Dad said. The recycler vent whined softly above him.

"This mission means I can go to Mendel!"

"Ana, there are more important things than getting what you want."

Frustration boiled over inside of me. "You don't want me to go to Earth, is that it?"

"Oh, Ana, that's not what I meant at all."

"What do I have to do to convince you that me going on this mission is a good thing?!"

Dad walked around the table and folded me into a hug. I kept my arms rigid and angry at my sides. "I'm sorry, Ana. But there's nothing you can do that will make me happy about sending my daughter off into mortal peril."

I STORMED out of the apartment. Dad didn't stop me. I deleted my report as I walked—wiped the whole thing. Useless.

I strode to Dr. Fletcher's apartment and buzzed.

She answered the door wearing well-worn slacks and a neatly patched blouse. "Ana, aren't you supposed to be in decompression?"

"Soon." I ran my thumb over the fraying cuff of my mylar sleeve. "Are you the reason why the hearing went to a vote?"

"Yes, it was your best chance to go."

At least one adult on this asteroid believed in me. I exhaled. "Thank you. I'll try to live up to all the trust you've put in me when I get to Mendel."

Dr. Fletcher smiled warmly. "You will. I'm so excited for you."

I tried to tell myself that her smile meant more to me than my father's disapproval.

CHAPTER 12

The room for getting suited up had its own shower. I grabbed one of the fist-sized mesh sacks on the wall and put it under the dry soap dispenser. A fine powder filled the bag. I scrubbed from my toes up, then flipped on the fan. Warm air shot down from the ceiling, and the recycling vent in the floor sucked at my toes. I brushed away the dry soap, then shook out my hair.

I flipped off the switch and exhaled. Right now, I didn't have the luxury of being upset at Dad or Cornelius. Suit up. Head to the mine shaft. Up the cage. Repair stuff. Reverse trip. I'd done it before. I could do it now—and get myself, Cornelius, and Zoe home safely.

I pulled on that obnoxious diaper and squeezed into my suit. Then I walked to the open area just in front of the airlock. Techs had set up benches with medical equipment. Lily Mason checked over every centimeter of my suit for tears, wear, or other problems while Nurse Hwang made sure the suit reported my vitals properly.

"Where's Mom?" I asked, glancing around. Dad wasn't there either.

"Oh." Nurse Hwang smiled apologetically. "Governor Cardoso thought it would look more professional if parents weren't involved. Dr. Kim made a good point about an IC investigation."

I groaned. Thanks, Dr. Kim.

"Don't worry. We've got you." Lily gave me an encouraging double-thumbs-up, then went back to examining my suit.

Maybe it was better this way. No more fights with Dad. No exhausted Mom yelling at Cornelius and me to play nice.

Zoe came out in her suit and sat on the next bench over. As soon as they finished with me, Lily and Nurse Hwang shifted to her. Zoe kept typing on the wristlet strapped over her suit, even as she had to turn this way and that for the suit check.

"What are you working on?" I asked.

"Website. Uploading photos."

"Oh. Maybe with this paycheck, plus your photos..." I began, knowing she wouldn't be able to buy a ticket to Earth this orbit but hoping she might make it next time around.

Zoe snorted. "Yeah, if my parents let me *keep* my paycheck."

I stared at her, stomach dropping. Nurse Hwang scanned her forehead with a thermometer, showing no sign of listening to our conversation.

"They're stealing it?"

"I'm a minor. It gets deposited into my parents' account. They've already told me how proud they are that I'm doing my part, blah blah blah, and how they've set up a research grant in my name and are awarding the whole thing back to the *Platinum Phoenix*. They're hoping it'll help us buy a second backup fab, but that's a pipe dream."

A twenty-thousand ICS paycheck was nothing compared to the ten million ICS price tag on a fabricator. What were her parents thinking? "I'm...I'm so sorry."

Zoe flicked her wristlet off. "Maybe if my pics didn't look like a prison, I'd get more donations."

"It's not quite the same as a prison," I offered, trying to cheer her up. But there wasn't a lot more I could say. "Aeroponics is nice."

"Aeroponics is a happy stain on the boringness of this death trap. You only think it's pretty because everything else here is so bland."

That afternoon nap hadn't done much for her. I almost repeated what Dr. Kim had told me about how the work in aeroponics was helping people back on Earth, but Zoe didn't seem like she wanted to be cheered up.

"I wish everything didn't suck for you," I said.

"Thanks." She gave me a sad smile. "Sorry, I'm so fun to be around right now."

"I'm not mad at you," I said.

"Yeah." Zoe cracked into a wry grin. "You don't really have a lot of other options for friends. Ditching me is a bad plan."

"That's not what I meant!"

"I know."

Then Cornelius walked in. He glanced nervously at me on his way to his bench. I scowled so he'd know I was still furious. Had he come for the paycheck? I could imagine him blowing it all on lame video game mods.

Lily and Nurse Hwang checked Cornelius too, then they helped us with our gloves. Techs ushered our parents in to hug us goodbye. Zoe pushed hers away. Part of me, spitefully, wanted to do the same, but my parents weren't stealing my pay, and I remembered the dark mines that were waiting for me. I hugged them both as tightly as I could through my stiff suit. As quickly as they'd been brought in, our parents were ushered back out.

Three techs snapped on our bubble helmets and 16-pound airpacks, full of eight hours of air. They checked and double-checked the air scrubber connections.

"Hey, good luck up there, kids," Lily said. "Final presents."

She handed me the diagnostics scanner and gave Cornelius the repair supply bag, leaving Zoe with the colony's last long-comm.

Daniel had suited up and stood at the airlock. His black, curly hair showed around the edges of his face. "I'll be taking you to the mine shaft. Ready?"

The small speaker in the back of my helmet carried his voice.

"Yes," I said. Zoe and Cornelius echoed me.

Daniel only managed a half-hearted grin—not at all like his usual, cheerful self. It seemed almost insulting that *he* was worried about all of this. He couldn't head up into the mines. Neither could his son Lucas—they were both far too tall. Daniel only had to escort us to the shaft.

The four of us stepped into the airlock. The aluminum-and-glass door slid shut, separating us from everyone else in the colony.

The air hissed as it was pulled through the vents. I flexed my fingers and breathed in the metallic-tasting air from my pack. I'd be out of this thing soon. Soon.

The far door opened silently. Daniel stepped out first. I strode after him, trying to look like I wasn't afraid. When I glanced over my shoulder, Cornelius and Zoe were right behind me. They hadn't hesitated, either.

We walked, the sounds of everyone's breathing echoing in my helmet. But my footfalls remained uncannily noiseless, just like before. It made me dizzy for a second—like my legs and brain weren't really in the same place.

I clambered into the large mine cart and sat flat against the back wall. Zoe and Cornelius glanced at the wheel wells.

"Trust me," I said. "You want to sit here."

Daniel joined us, too. "Hey, Lily. Go ahead and start the cart."

We jerked forward. Zoe yawned again, determined to be cool—either that, or she was about to nod off. Had she even tried to sleep this afternoon? Cornelius got all wide-eyed and pale-faced, his lips pursed tight. Pity soured my stomach. He didn't belong here. At all.

I leaned closer to him, not that he needed me closer to hear. "You all right?"

"Fine." His unsteady voice crackled through my speaker.

Zoe made a disgusted face at him. I wanted to snap at her, but our comms were connected—all the way back to the ISRU techs. The cart sped past blasted, red-brown rock. I couldn't do anything to help Cornelius. Just then, I felt Dad's words in my bones—I was a tiny part of a huge universe I didn't know nearly enough about.

The cart slowed. That short, slender, silvery cage waited for us with the door lowered to form a ramp.

"Who's first?" Daniel asked as we lurched to a halt.

"Me." I could at least be waiting for Zoe and Cornelius when they reached the top after that cramped, lonely ride. "Oh! Zoe and Cornelius. Do you have any music downloaded on your wristlets?"

"What?" Cornelius asked. Zoe's eyes widened, then she quickly tapped a few buttons on her wristlet.

"To listen to on the way up," Zoe said. "Great idea."

"I should have remembered sooner." I tapped on my wristlet, saving some files from the colony cloud to its limited hard drive. "Cornelius, you come next. Zoe, take the rear."

Zoe grinned. She couldn't stop bouncing her foot like she was excited. Weird. I guess it was better than freaking out like Jayden and puking inside her helmet.

I walked up the ramp, tilting my head to fit inside the tight space. For the first time ever, I was grateful for my steady diet of algae. If I'd had more food to grow on, I probably wouldn't have fit.

Daniel closed the door. From here on out, we kids were on our own.

CHAPTER 13

Acceleration pushed against my feet as the cage lifted me upward. Zoe, Cornelius, and Daniel kept talking, but Zoe was the one with the long-comm, not me. Their voices disappeared after a minute or so.

"Wristlet," I said. "Play *The Sound of Music*."

My elbows and knees ached from pressing against the cage. It was smaller than I remembered—or I was bigger. But at least I could close my eyes this time and pretend I was twirling, arms stretched wide with the Alps behind me, just like Julie Andrews did in the movie. Soon enough, I'd be on Earth, with a blue sky above and green grass underfoot.

Lily Mason had recommended the movie during one of our Tuesday workshops. She'd gotten the whole idea of reusing mylar blankets to sew kids' clothes from a scene where Maria cut up curtains.

I could almost ignore the weight of kilometers of rock all around me when I thought about Maria's problems instead of my own.

What would it be like to have curtains? Or *windows*?

The cage slowed to a stop. The door soundlessly swung down into a ramp. The mines gaped before me, only illuminated by a streak of light from my headlamp. I didn't even have the long-comm for company.

I sat on the ramp, rubbed my tingling legs, and stretched my neck. I wasn't falling over and damaging my air scrubber again, even if Cornelius and Zoe would be here soon. After a few minutes, I stood and shuffled down the ramp, trying to get used to the springy feel of moving in ninety percent gravity. As soon as I closed the cage, it lowered soundlessly into the shaft. I peered down the hole, watching as it turned into a silver speck. I'd fall for a long, long time if I tripped into the shaft.

A bit woozy, I edged away and sat with my back against the mine wall. I turned my head, sweeping the headlamp's light across the open room. There, not four meters away, hunkered the shifter. The squat machine was two meters wide, with a tread and scoop like a bulldozer, plus sweeper arms on both sides.

My light cast long, teeth-shaped shadows over it. Behind the shifter, I could just make out a pillar of intact rock, left to support the low, rough ceiling. The whole room still looked alien to me. My breathing accelerated.

I turned my head and watched the cage cables whirl instead, trying to inhale the music of green hills, alive with music. I didn't have to get used to the vacuum-silence, darkness, or strange gravity. I'd be home tonight. And to Mendel a few weeks after that.

I listened to everyone sing about their favorite things and pretended that sitting alone in a hollowed-out chunk of asteroid wasn't any creepier than a thunderstorm. Maybe thunderstorms were worse, I tried to tell myself. It's not like I'd ever been in one.

The cage eventually returned. I scrambled to my feet. Cornelius stumbled out, but I caught and steadied him. One arm still holding on to him, I closed the cage.

He spoke, pausing my music. "This is...spookier than I thought it would be." He swallowed hard, looking around with wide, terrified eyes.

I wanted to send him straight back to the safety of the colony. Why hadn't he listened to me?

"You shouldn't have come," I snapped.

He pulled away. "I wanted to."

"For the sake of coming? This is dangerous!"

His head shrunk toward his shoulders. "You're here."

"Of course I'm here! I'm trying to get to *Earth*. What are you doing?"

He didn't answer. I didn't push him. Zoe would be coming into range soon, and I didn't want her overhearing this.

I sat against the wall again and turned *The Sound of Music* back on. Cornelius didn't interrupt. He stared at that narrow shaft, hugging the repair kit to his chest, his back pressed against the wall next to me.

When the cage reappeared and the door opened, Zoe paused to rub her legs down like a veteran pro. She strode out, grinning. "Ready?"

Her peppy tone annoyed me, but it shouldn't have. At least she seemed awake now. "Yes." The sooner we fixed the shifter, the sooner we could leave. "Zoe, I need you to get the long-comm up and transmitting to the techs. Once they can get data from us, I'll look the shifter over with the diagnostic scanner."

"Do you want me to do something?" Cornelius asked.

"No." He ought to be at home, playing his games and waiting for me to get back. Like last time, when I knew that finishing the mission meant he'd be safe—even if I didn't return.

Zoe and I waddled toward the shifter, leaving Cornelius against the wall. She unclipped the long-comm from her belt and powered it up. Daniel had taught us that it shot weak pulses through the cage cable that acted like a super-sophisticated Morse code. The machines up here all communicated that way, but our wristlets and the diagnostic scanner couldn't do it, and their signals weren't powerful enough to punch through the rock by themselves.

"Is it running?" I asked Zoe.

"Sure."

I started up the diagnostic scanner, then circled the shifter, looking for a likely place to start scanning once the long-comm connected us to the techs. When I got to the far side, I froze. I didn't need a fancy tool to tell what had gone wrong. All the tiny, star-shaped screws in one of the panels had been removed and tossed on the ground, along with the panel itself. Clean-cut wires dangled out of the hole, like flopping spaghetti noodles.

The shifter hadn't malfunctioned. It didn't need some routine maintenance.

This was sabotage.

CHAPTER 14

I couldn't keep my voice steady. "Zoe, I need the long-comm over here to relay this to the techs."

Zoe tapped on the long-comm screen, then strolled over as smoothly as she could in the lower-g. She stared at the cut wires. "Whoa, what a mess."

I lifted the scanner, but the green transmission light didn't turn on. I tapped the screen—fully charged, as I'd thought. Maybe it hadn't finished booting yet?

My gaze drifted back to those snipped wires. Sabotage. Who would do that to us, to this asteroid? My stomach churned. Space was dangerous. We were supposed to keep each other alive out here. Everyone on the *Platinum Phoenix* shared that goal.

At least, I thought we did until about five minutes ago.

I tapped the scanner again. Broken. Not transmitting. How had the techs missed that?

Cornelius' voice cut into my helmet. "Is that your website?"

"Yup," Zoe said.

I whipped around. Cornelius had walked up next to Zoe while I wasn't watching. She was typing on the long-comm; it wasn't in scanner-relay mode at all. Nothing was wrong with my equipment.

"What are you doing?" I demanded.

"This is the most interesting thing I've had to photograph

in...well, ever. It'll double my views, easy." She gave me a flat look. "Some of us need to be creative to *earn* our way to Earth."

I jerked back a step. How could she think I hadn't worked for my paycheck? Was she jealous? I wanted to defend myself, but I swallowed back a sharp reply. Zoe was slowing down the mission. We could bicker about who'd earned what later. She'd already posted a half-dozen clear, crisp photos of the sabotaged cables and the scattered star-shaped screws—she must have taken them with the long-comm while I was trying to get the stupid scanner to work.

"We need to get our job done and get home," I said. "Are you even allowed to post those?"

Zoe shrugged. "They're going through the colony's antennae just fine."

That wasn't the same thing.

"I order you to stop. I'm mission leader, and—"

Zoe wrinkled her nose. "Geez, this place sure makes you tense. They're posted now. Changing over to scanner-relay, Your Highness."

How could she be so calm up here? Our suits could rip, our oxygen could run out, the mine could collapse, or a hundred other things. A mission wasn't the time for some recreational blogging.

Dad should have lectured her about taking things seriously, not me. I didn't need words to explain how deadly the mines could be. I had memories to remind me. Up here, it was hard not to think about the weight that had pressed on my lungs or how leaden my arms had been. The sooner we got back down, the better.

I held out the scanner. Blue strings of light flickered all over the shifter, the chopped wires, and the dusty exterior. Eerie. Ghost-like.

The blue light faded back down to nothingness in a few minutes.

"And now we wait. I'm so glad we got the scan sent *right away*." Zoe's voice dripped sarcasm. She tapped the long-comm screen back over to her website. Apparently, she'd kept it running in the background because she squealed, "Oooh! I've got comments! I wasn't expecting any so fast, not with our lag."

"Maybe you should take that down. Before it spreads further," I said. "That's evidence. I don't know if it's wise—"

"You're my mission leader," Zoe said, "but you can't give me orders about my website. We'll be back in the colony in an hour or two, and then you can cry to my parents. Okay?"

Frustration tightened my muscles. I was also her friend—at least I thought I was. "I wasn't threatening to get you in trouble; I was trying to keep you *out of it*. We could ask Dr. Fletcher. She likes both of us, and she knows about asteroid policies and stuff."

"Did...did you say *evidence?*" Cornelius fumbled.

I'd almost forgotten he was here. He hunched behind Zoe, eyes wide. He reminded me of the trembling baby capybara in the nature documentary we'd watched last week—the creature had ended up as an anaconda's lunch.

"It's nothing," I said. Apparently, he hadn't figured it out, and I didn't want to scare him.

He peered at me, then the wires. "Evidence of what?"

"Someone cut them," Zoe chimed in. "Snip, snip. Do you think they left any other traps up here?"

Zoe didn't even look up as she spoke; she kept typing with her thumbs on the long-comm. In some other situation, I would have been impressed with how well she did that in her gloves.

Cornelius looked at me. "Is that true?"

I sighed. "Stay calm. We'll be done soon. Zoe, do you have the repair instructions yet?"

"Yup, it's pretty simple. Patch the wires." She tapped some buttons, uploading the data from the long-comm to my wristlet. "The techs called Governor Cardoso and CEO Yun. Given all the snipping, he's called an emergency meeting with the board to decide if they should have us finish the mission or call us back down immediately."

We were paid as contractors for *completed* work. No repair meant no paycheck. By the time they finished arguing, I could have this thing done.

"Patch me to the technicians. I need them to talk me through this," I said.

"Yes, Your Majesty."

I bit back a tart retort. Now wasn't the time.

Zoe tapped some things on the long-comm, and Daniels' voice streamed into my helmet. "You kids all right up there?"

"Fine."

"Any other signs of—"

"Not that I can see. I know there's a meeting going on, but I'm not sitting on my butt while they squabble. Can you help me through this?"

"Absolutely!" Daniel said, sounding like his cheerful self again. "The long-comm's relaying video from your wristlet. If you make a mistake, I'm right here to correct you."

I'd spliced wires thousands of times during the Tuesday workshops, but I was grateful to have Daniel double-checking my work.

"First thing," Daniel said. "Check the side panel and make sure the shifter's turned off."

I walked around to the other side, even though I'd already seen the dead panel. The circle of light from my headlamp confirmed it was still off. "We're good."

"All right. Preheat the soldering iron."

"Cornelius, soldering iron."

He fumbled with his pack and then handed me the wire strippers with a hopeful smile. Of course he hadn't learned the names of any of this stuff.

"I'll need those next. Here." I pulled out the soldering iron—a stick a little longer than my hand with a metal tip—along with its stand. I flicked on its switch.

Daniel spoke again. "We'll work from left to right, just like writing, okay?"

I managed not to roll my eyes. I knew my left hand from my right hand. "Okay."

"Do you see the pair with the blue coating? Strip those."

I did, revealing two centimeters of fine, coppery wires on each side.

"Remember to slip on a piece of heat shrink next," Daniel said. "Then solder the wires together."

I'd already grabbed the heat shrink. After snipping off a piece and sliding it down the wire out of the way, I gripped the sections I'd stripped. The glove's textured fingers let me pull each side into a tight bundle, then twist them into each other. I didn't ask Cornelius for the spool of gray solder—I pulled it out myself.

I held the iron to the bottom of the wires, getting them nice and hot. Then I touched the top of them with a thread of solder. The heated-up wire melted the solder, and it ran over the splice, turning it silvery. I pulled the heat shrink over it, then melted the plastic smooth with a mini heat gun. Now it couldn't cross with other wires, and it wasn't likely to short out. "Done."

"Good," Daniel said. "Do you see the green wires? You need to splice those back together, too."

I repeated the process. As we moved to the third wire, his voice weakened to a crackle. I caught every third word: "...great...purple...next."

I frowned. The long-comm should be freshly charged. "Zoe?"

"Doing fine."

I frowned—that wasn't what I meant. I stepped around the shifter. Zoe sat near the shaft, thumbs flying again. The cage hung next to her on its cables, half a meter above the shaft, its ramp still open and extended down.

"This is no time for updating your site!"

Daniel crackled in, "...there?"

"I'm sitting right by the shaft," Zoe said. "The long-comm should be strong enough for you to get babied through repairs and let me reply to my comments."

"Well, it isn't! How many comments could you possibly have?" I demanded. How could she think of her comments right now? Even if I didn't like living on the asteroid, I understood I was part of the colony, which meant doing my best to keep everyone alive. After thirteen years of living together here, she ought to know that, too.

"Seventy-seven." Zoe's thumbs kept going. "But given our horrible lag here, it could be double that, easy. I've made twenty-five ICS in new donations, thanks for asking. Think I'll get to Earth soon?"

I hadn't thought she could be this petty. I hated that she couldn't buy a ticket to Earth, but I steeled myself to sound like her leader and not her friend. "Stop it. They can wait; this can't."

Zoe didn't stop.

I exhaled through my nose. We'd never get the repairs done like this. I stomped over—difficult in the lower-g—and stuck out my hand. "Give me the long-comm. Cornelius is taking over your job."

"You're such a tyrant!"

"Hand it over." I wanted to kick her in the shins. "We're

doing this mission, and we're doing it right. Then we can go home."

"Fine! You're so...so..." Zoe gestured wildly with both arms, exasperated. Her hand holding the long-comm struck the bottom of the cage.

"Ow!" Zoe shouted.

She dropped the long-comm.

Our only source of communication with the colony fell down the shaft, bouncing noiselessly against the sides. Down, down, down.

My brain expected a thundering crash, but all I heard was Daniel's faint voice. "Hello? Is something..."

And then that disappeared, too, and I was left with the deafening silence of space.

CHAPTER 15

Two and a half kilometers. The long-comm fell for two and a half kilometers, banging down a narrow hole. Even if it didn't shatter into a thousand pieces, there was no way it wouldn't be broken beyond repair. Not without a fab to fix it. And the colony didn't have another one.

"Oops," Zoe said as if she'd dropped a pencil instead of breaking one of the most valuable pieces of equipment on the asteroid.

"I told you to stop writing!" I shouted, frizzing the speakers.

Zoe rolled her eyes. "I've stopped now. Are you happy?"

"Go sit somewhere where you can't hurt anything else," I ordered. "Including yourself. By the support pillar would be good." I waved at the shadowy shape on the other side of the shifter.

For the first time, Zoe looked scared. "Aren't we...I mean... shouldn't we just go back?"

"I came here to do a mission. We're only here because everyone voted that this mission was necessary. What's going back now going to accomplish? There's not another long-comm. So shut up and sit still."

I stormed back to the far side of the shifter, not caring if she actually moved away from the shaft. I stripped the wires and tossed the colorful plastic on the floor.

Cornelius shuffled next to me and cleared his throat. "Umm...shouldn't we...isn't Zoe...right?"

"I'm finishing this. Heat-shrink."

"You don't have Daniel anymore," he said, voice strengthening. Calm, level. Reasonable. It made him sound like Dad.

I shook my head as if that could clear the sound. "Then I'll carry on without him. I know how to do this. I still have the schematic downloaded, and even if I didn't, it's easy. I just match up the cut wires. Where's my heat-shrink?"

Cornelius still didn't move. "If the colony actually gets close to running out of water, then we'll come fix it."

"Heat-shrink! Is that so hard?" I brushed past him and grabbed it out of the bag. "You make a big fuss about coming, and now you're sitting there like a lump. Why aren't you back at home playing video games? Did you think this would be fun?"

"No! I think it's scary and that we should go back. It's the safe thing to do. The smart thing to do." Cornelius gestured at the shaft. Zoe had moved away from it—her helmet made a puddle of light next to the support pillar.

Her voice buzzed into the conversation. "I'm with Corny."

He bristled, and so did I. Only I got to call my brother that. I wished I had a way to mute her out of our conversation.

"Too bad for both of you that this isn't a democracy," I said. "Take the cage back down if you like. Let everyone else know that you're cowards who can't follow orders." I shoved the heat-shrink over one wire, wrenched the coppery bits together, soldered, yanked the heat-shrink down, and applied the heat gun. On to the next wire.

"All you care about is your dumb paycheck," Cornelius said.

My jaw tensed, but I kept stripping wires. I was going to finish my mission, just like last time. Wasn't that the right thing to do, whether or not I got paid?

He scowled. "The mines aren't safe, you know."

"Then leave! I'll follow in twenty minutes."

"You hate the *Platinum Phoenix* that much?" Cornelius demanded.

There was plenty I liked about this rock. Aeroponics. Family dinner. My friends. But that didn't mean I wanted to live here forever.

"I came here to do this mission, just like the hearing decided. I'm not going back until it's finished."

"Until you have your money!" Cornelius spat. "Money, money, money. Paycheck, paycheck, paycheck. I hate you."

He stormed over to Zoe and plunked down next to her.

Fine. They could both sit there and mope. I didn't need help to finish this; I had the supplies and skills to do it myself. Tapping the side of my helmet, I turned my light to maximum.

Strip. Twist. Solder. Heat-shrink. Repeat. Repeat. Repeat. My muscles tightened into knots up my arms to the base of my neck. This was all Zoe's fault. She should have handed me the long-comm. She was supposed to be my friend and my one dependable crewmate, but she'd thrown a tantrum instead.

My fingers ached from all the fine work in my stiff suit, but I stretched them and continued, matching the colors, the wires, occasionally checking the instructions still uploaded to my wristlet to make sure I was doing it right.

Strip. Twist. Solder. Heat-shrink. The wires waved in front of my eyes, and I blinked hard to steady myself. It would have been easier with Daniel double-checking my work. Stupid Zoe. Even another set of hands from my crewmembers would have helped. I glanced at them. Zoe had closed her eyes, but her foot shook nervously, so she wasn't asleep. Cornelius hugged his knees. Somehow, he'd already gotten his white suit dusty.

Strip. Twist. Solder. I finished the last one. Done. I stretched out my neck and my fingers. "I'm turning it on to make sure it works. Then we'll head out."

"Finally," Zoe muttered, almost too soft to hear.

I wanted to snap at her, but I bit my tongue. No point in starting another fight when we were nearly finished. We'd head down the shaft in a few minutes.

I booted up the side panel.

Something sparked at the back of the machine. Before I could power it down, the shifter's treads jerked forward. I shrieked and jumped away.

The shifter rammed ahead into the wall, right over the shaft that could take us back to the colony. The machine crumpled the cage, like it was nothing more than an algae foil.

The wires I'd fixed sparked once more, then went dead.

I crept forward, the hairs on my neck raised. The side panel was powered off. I circled to one side of the shifter, then the other. I tried to pull the cage out, but it was pinned. Even if I could get it out, what use would it be, smashed like that?

I crawled under the shifter, looking for a different angle—something that might help. I only saw something worse: the tread of the shifter covered the shaft entirely.

"Is it bad?" Cornelius asked. He and Zoe headed toward me, their lights bobbing over the rock.

I didn't answer. I crawled back out and tried to push the shifter, but of course, I couldn't move the heavy equipment. Ten adults probably couldn't budge it.

My palms turned clammy, and I had nowhere to wipe them.

I looked over the wires. Had I failed to wrap one of them well enough? Had I crossed something? I couldn't even tell where they'd been sparking.

Maybe if I turned the shifter back on, I could get it working. I reached for the panel.

"Are you nuts?" Zoe's voice lanced through my helmet. "How do you think that's going to help?"

"I'm trying to move it," I said, voice tight. "The shaft's blocked."

"Yeah, even if it doesn't freak out again and crush us, how are we going to get back? We can't climb down that."

She was right. We couldn't climb two and a half kilometers down a vertical shaft. We'd make it to the bottom—the asteroid's artificial gravity would see to that—but we wouldn't be alive to enjoy it.

I took three deep breaths. Panicking wasn't an option. I was the oldest, and I had to take care of us. Make sure we somehow got home safe.

We were trapped. And it was my fault.

CHAPTER 16

"You're an idiot," Zoe said as soon as she reached the shaft and saw the damage.

"I'm not the one who dropped the long-comm." We wouldn't be stuck up here if Daniel had been checking my work. "I told you that you shouldn't have been working on your website."

"Wow, a bit of typing did not cause this. You had to be annoying and nag me. If you—"

"I was trying to finish our mission!"

Cornelius shuffled toward us. He looked over the shifter, the crunched cage, everything, and his face sagged. "I just wanted to go home."

Zoe turned on him. "You think the rest of us were planning on a tea party up here? You're an idiot, too, Corny."

"Don't call me that!"

"Both of you, stop fighting." I needed to think, but my brain felt like it was boiling, all the good thoughts bursting and vanishing into steam before I could grasp them. "We're going to survive this."

"How?" Zoe demanded.

I looked over the wreck again. The cables that lifted and lowered the cage still seemed intact—they'd let out slack instead of snapping when the shifter hit.

"The techs will be worried about us. Right now, they're probably sending Daniel back out to check the bottom of the shaft. From his perspective, it'll look like we've only dropped the long-comm. They won't be able to see that the shaft is covered. I can use the soldering iron to write a message on the cloth of the supply bag and drop it down. When they find it, they'll know to send up another cage."

"To drop a message or bring up a cage, we'll have to get the shifter off the shaft." Zoe folded her arms and glared at me. "You're an idiot."

"Do you have any better ideas?" I demanded. "Whining about this isn't helping."

Zoe said nothing. Finally.

"I want both of you to stand back while I try to turn this thing on," I said.

That didn't take much encouragement; they retreated behind the squat pillar and crouched behind it.

I took a deep breath, then tapped the panel.

Nothing happened.

I tried again. I jammed my fingers against that blank, gray screen, waiting for something to happen. Nothing. Not even a flicker of light.

"It's dead," I whispered, knowing they'd hear me just fine.

One of them sucked in a scared breath, but neither of them said anything. "I'm going to check on the mining machinery. Maybe we can use one of them to move the shifter. Or just tear it up. Will both of you stay there?"

"Yes," they said in unison. I tried not to envy them as they sat down by the pillar. They wouldn't be walking into the darkness.

Lily sent a map of the mines to my wristlet before we left. I tapped it up, blue lines glowing across the white sleeve of my suit. The current excavation site was close. Command had decided to mine near the shaft for the time being in case kids needed to make repairs. Less travel time. All the mining equipment would be there, but not actively mining—progress had stopped when the shifter broke down.

The stout pillar by Zoe and Cornelius disappeared long before the next one showed up, leaving me in a sea of ink cut only by the long shaft of my headlamp. Sometimes the low ceiling knocked into my helmet, but I didn't shriek this time. I focused on walking without falling on my face in this reduced gravity.

I knew I should dim my helmet. The full-strength light was for delicate repair work. But I couldn't bring myself to mute one watt of the brightness cutting across the red-brown stone. The rocks looked like millennia-old rust. Or blood. But I tried not to think about blood, aliens, or the crushing mass of the rocks above me as I pressed forward. I was on the *Platinum Phoenix*. These were just mining galleries. I was just one kid on a failed repair mission, trying to get home.

I froze where I stood. *Failed.* No paycheck. No Earth. I'd be spending at least the next orbit—two years—on this asteroid. My lungs rattled. No Earth. No Mendel Academy. No running through the grasses of the Pampas.

"What happened?" Cornelius' soft voice drifted into the speaker, a lifeline. "Your breathing sounds odd."

"I, umm, stubbed my toe. It's hard to walk in this gravity." I couldn't explain why I'd actually stopped. "I'm halfway to the mining equipment. What do things look like by you?"

"Same as before. Dark. Big shifter on top of our way home," Cornelius said.

"Zoe hasn't run off?"

Her voice cut in. "I can hear you, you know."

"I'm glad you're safe," Cornelius said, his voice as close in my helmet as if he was standing behind me. "I thought the saboteur might have jumped you."

My throat tightened. I glanced in every direction but saw no one. "D-do you think the saboteur is still up here?"

"How would I know?" Cornelius asked.

I moved slower, turning my head from side to side, trying to illuminate as much ground as possible. In the curve of every shadow, I imagined a crouching figure in a spacesuit with a knife, waiting to attack me—to leave my guts dangling out of me, just like the shifters. Except I couldn't solder human insides back together.

Who was I kidding? I couldn't even solder the shifter's guts together. "Cornelius, keep talking to me."

"About what?"

"I don't care!" Hearing my brother made me feel less alone. Less vulnerable. "What's the last video game you downloaded?"

"*Dragons vs. Rockets*. It's another racing game. You, umm, want to hear about it right now?"

"Yes, talk. Please."

Sabotaging the shifter seemed like the work of a madman. It didn't make sense. My light rolled over the rock, casting weird shadows everywhere.

Why would anyone sabotage us? Purposefully try to stop the mining operations?

Something caught the edge of my vision. I glanced right. Had something moved? No, I'd just glimpsed an odd-shaped lump of stone. If I didn't calm down, I'd start shaking and throw up like Jayden had.

Cornelius cheerfully explained the pros and cons of racing a dragon or a rocket. There were cyborg-dragons, too, but Cornelius thought their middle-of-the-road stats sadly weren't worth playing.

I clung to his words. My brother's voice made the shadows less alive and the rock more innocent.

I couldn't get jumpy. I had to be the leader. If the saboteur attacked us, I needed to fight back and give Zoe and Cornelius a chance to hide somewhere safe. As safe as they could be in these mines, with only so much oxygen strapped on their backs. My headlamp cast snaking shadows around the upcoming pillar. Thankfully, no huge, hulking monster lurked behind it.

And that's when it struck me. The saboteur couldn't be some deranged adult. Adults didn't fit up the shafts. That's why we'd come up to do repairs in the first place.

The saboteur was a kid.

My pounding pulse pressed hard against the counter-pressure of my suit. I tried to keep my breathing the same. It wouldn't help to freak Cornelius and Zoe out. Thankfully, Cornelius was lost in talking about his game. I pictured everyone's desks at school. No one had been absent this morning. The saboteur had to be one of my classmates, but they weren't up here now.

I reached the mining machinery and saw the charge-setter first, but I couldn't blow up the shifter. An explosion would destroy the cage pulley system, too. Maybe a chewer could do the job? They smoothed the floor after blasts, keeping everything clean for other machines' tread. It would probably ruin their cutting teeth to eat through the shifter, but I'd rather destroy some equipment than stay up here.

I tried to boot up its side panel.

Nothing.

I tried again. Just like the shifter, it wouldn't turn on. Punching the panel only bruised my knuckles.

"Ana?" Cornelius asked, pausing his explanation of the various racing tracks mid-sentence.

"The robots won't turn on. The techs know we're up here, but they don't know where we are anymore. They've locked the machines into shut-down."

"They're trying to keep us safe," Zoe whispered. "Prevent an accident."

They wouldn't turn the machines on unless they got our

message. And we couldn't send a message without the machines.

Which one of my classmates did this to us?

"Don't the machines all have some kind of long-comm?" Cornelius asked. "That's how the techs control them, right? Can we hack into one of those?"

I laughed, bitter and dry. "Even if they weren't powered down, I don't even know if that's possible, let alone how to do it. They weren't designed for human input. There's a reason we brought the long-comm."

No response. I circled the useless machines, looking for something I could pry loose and use as a crowbar to move the shifter. As if my team weighed enough for that to work. I was just delaying defeat now.

"I'm headed back toward you. Stay put."

"Like we have anywhere to go," Zoe mumbled.

I wished I could have muted that. Cornelius stopped talking about *Dragons vs. Robots*, and I didn't trust my voice to ask him to keep going. The lump in my throat tasted like a brick of algae. A kid I knew cut those wires. Now we were stuck. And I couldn't get us out. I checked my wristlet. 2138. We'd stepped into the mine over two hours ago. That meant we each had less than six hours of oxygen left. Less than six hours until we suffocated. For the first time, I wished that my airpack straps felt *heavier*.

I tried to breathe shallowly, but I gulped in air, cold panic itching down my neck. I was the oldest—I knew space was dangerous. And I'd decided to stay and try to fix the shifter myself anyway. Zoe dropping the long-comm was bad, but I'd had a choice. I'd made that choice for all of us.

Now we'd all eat the consequences.

I collapsed next to Zoe and Cornelius, my legs shaking, even though the walk hadn't been that hard. Zoe watched me expectantly.

But I had no ideas. We couldn't move the shifter with our hands or send any messages. Zoe would never get to finish responding to all those comments. Right now, I actually felt bad about that.

Cornelius turned toward me. The gathered light of three headlamps glared off the floor. "What now?"

I couldn't even rub the side of my aching face through my helmet. Dad had warned me about being overconfident, and he'd been right. I'd underestimated the dangers of space. I'd thought I was strong, even when he'd reminded me that there's so much we don't understand yet.

I'd failed to understand wires.

"You don't have a plan, do you?" Cornelius asked.

"No."

He squirmed. "I...was hoping you did."

Me too.

He kept fidgeting. Odd. I'd expected him to cry. "Cornelius...do *you* have an idea?"

"Umm. Kind of."

"Why didn't you say something?" I wasn't sure if I wanted to hug him or slap the back of his helmet.

He shrunk back against the pillar. "Because I really don't like it."

# CHAPTER 17

"I like any plan better than—" I almost said *than dying*, but I bit my tongue. We might actually die up here. That familiar, crushing fear crept back over my lungs. Once the *Platinum Phoenix* bought supplies from Earth to fix the fab, would the repair robots push our corpses back down the shaft? Or would we sit here forever, lifelessly watching the machines mine as they returned to work?

I really didn't want to die.

I gulped in my stale, recycled oxygen. I knew it was limited, but I couldn't stop myself. "I like any plan better than just sitting still. What is it?"

"There's one more mineshaft," Cornelius said. "We could try to go down it."

How had I overlooked that? The engineers had originally carved out three shafts so that if one failed, mining could continue. The exploding charge-setter had destroyed one of them, and we'd capped this one, but that still left a singular shaft and a way home.

Cornelius wasn't useless up here, after all.

I tapped my wristlet and pulled up the map again. We sat in a roughly square-shaped room, two kilometers to a side, with our shaft against one wall. Plenty of galleries shot out from it, but the one we needed was on the corner farthest away from us. That narrow gallery stretched for three kilometers before reaching an open, one-kilometer square room. A strange, squiggly line arched across the space near the gallery entrance. The shaft was another quarter-kilometer away, over the line.

Maybe the squiggle was a valuable vein of ore? Or ice? I couldn't recall Mom talking about any machinery working there, even before the fab broke. Whatever that line represented, it couldn't be worse than standing here and waiting to die.

"How far is it?" Zoe asked, leaning over my shoulder. She bumped me, blurring the image.

"Five kilometers."

"*Five?* Are you nuts? I'm staying here."

I pursed my lips and stared at the map. Five kilometers. In the rec hall, at a casual walk, I did a kilometer in ten minutes, easy. We might go a bit slower over a long distance with the lowered-g making everything awkward. But even if we walked twice as slow, we'd make it in under two hours.

"It's a good plan, Cornelius," I said. "Thanks."

He beamed like I'd promised to make him a birthday present every day for the rest of his life.

"Wander out there? In the *mines?*" Zoe's voice jumped an octave. "Where it's dark, and...and..."

Now she got scared? "The techs have locked down the mining equipment. Nothing's going to hit us. We can't get down this shaft. But the other shaft will have a cage—one that isn't broken. It's our only way home."

Zoe shook her head, staring at me with huge eyes. "It's dark out there, and it's creepy."

"There's nothing else up here. Nothing to be afraid of," I assured her, even as cold dread hollowed my stomach. I had to set a good example and stay calm. The only thing worse than underestimating the dangers of space was panicking. "Zoe, think about this. How long do you think it will take the adults to figure out what's wrong, clear the shaft, and send up a new cage?"

Zoe frowned, forehead scrunched. "Maybe a day. Or two?"

Well, at least she still had some optimism left. The techs might be able to do something before the colony got a new fabricator, but I wouldn't place any bets on it.

Cornelius groaned. "We don't have any food!"

"He's right." Worse, we didn't have enough oxygen. But if I reminded Zoe about it, she might freak and hyperventilate. "It's not so bad, Zoe. Just a walk. Like strolling around the rec hall. Five kilometers, you can do that. Even if we take it super-slow, we'll be at the shaft in two hours and home in three—long before the techs even figure out what went wrong."

We had twice as much time as we needed. I clung to that.

Zoe turned the color of dead algae. "This wasn't supposed to happen."

"Accidents never are. But we'll make it through this."

She didn't stand; she was trembling. I'd expected Cornelius to flip out, not her. Zoe had been so relaxed while scanning the sabotage and the loss of the long-comm.

"Cornelius, help me," I said. We each took one of her arms and pulled her up. Our headlamps cut three long lines across the reddish rock and the too-low ceiling before fading into darkness.

Maybe Zoe needed a job—something to focus on. "Zoe, each of the big pillars we'll pass has a microtag. I'll watch the map," I pulled it up on my wristlet, "but I need you to scan the pillars with your wristlet and tell me their number, all right?"

She nodded, silent. When we started moving, she followed as quickly as a robot with tread on only one side. Maybe Zoe needed something to talk about, too. She'd seemed so happy while she was typing.

"You'll have a great story for your website when we get back." I tried to inject cheerfulness into my voice. "I bet you have three hundred comments by now."

"I can't reply to comments."

"No, but your readers are in suspense. After we're home safe, you can tell them that you were in a pinch, but it all worked out."

Zoe paused, steps faltering. "If we all die up here...the internet would go ballistic, wouldn't it?"

Okay, so talking about her site wasn't a good idea. Cornelius flinched. "You think we're going to die?"

Words I'd so carefully avoided saying. "We're all going to be fine. Let's keep walking."

"Sabotage is bad on its own. Probably bad enough for the IC to get involved. Three kids' corpses..." Zoe hugged her arms to her chest. "They'd open child protection cases for sure. For everyone left, that is."

At least Zoe's complaints gave me something other than my sore legs to think about. The stiff suit and the off gravity weren't doing me any favors. "I don't think the IC will get involved. They decided not to do anything about the colony sending me up."

"But they thought about it. Three kids, plus sabotage, plus a lost long-comm? Yeah, the IC will care about us for once. They'll notice," Zoe said.

Cornelius' brow scrunched. "What...what would happen if the IC opened cases and stuff?"

"They could just whisk us away. Take us from our parents," Zoe said, as though that would be amazing. "They might send us to the Lunar Colonies at first, but custody trials take so long, they'd have to ship us to Earth."

IC law didn't let minors stay on the moon for more than two months—effects of low-g on growing bodies and all. I shuddered, imagining all the kids ripped away from their families and homes.

Zoe sighed. "Wouldn't that be nice? A free trip to Earth for all the kids. Not just you and your paychecks, Ana."

"I'm not getting paid for this mission." But even without pay, could I still get to Mendel? My chest ached. If the IC took me to Earth, they'd let me stay once I was there, wouldn't they?

"Would the IC put everyone, our whole family, into protective custody?" Cornelius asked.

"Idiot. No one puts adults under protective custody," Zoe snorted.

Cornelius fidgeted with the tips of his gloves. "If they only take us...won't all the parents try to follow? If lots of adults try to leave...I don't think our colony can keep working. We need everyone. The whole asteroid could empty out."

"So?" Zoe asked.

"I don't want the *Platinum Phoenix* to die." Cornelius shook his head. "I hope the IC never hears about this."

"Bah! Who cares about this asteroid? It's a lump of rock!" Zoe's tone brightened as she ranted. "It's never going to make money again. Everything broke this orbit because we didn't have enough profit for proper supplies. It's about time the IC cared that there are a bunch of kids locked up on this death trap. Did you want to come? Did you sign your name to be here?"

"I was born here," Cornelius said defensively.

"Exactly."

I frowned. I didn't want to live here, but thinking of this asteroid as an evacuated shell made me wilt. When I was at Mendel, I wanted to read articles about how aeroponics was helping with the Kansas, USA droughts. I wanted notes from Mom about the cool stuff they'd mined. I wanted Dae-sung to send me his latest, impossible plans for a zero-g rec hall. I didn't want the saboteur to ruin everyone else's lives.

"Ana...if the IC took us away, Mom and Dad would follow, right? We'd still be together?" Cornelius whispered.

Would the IC transport them to Earth for an investigation?

Or would our parents have to pay? We were only close to buying one ticket, not two. And that was assuming our parents chose to leave the *Platinum Phoenix* behind for us.

My helmet knocked against another rough patch. A headache threatened between my eyes.

"I don't want anything to tear our family apart," Cornelius whimpered.

Zoe barked a laugh. "Stop being such a baby. There's a whole planet of people on Earth. I wouldn't worry about the handful you might leave behind."

I bristled. I liked a lot of that handful of people—including my parents.

We neared one of those huge, stout support pillars. "Zoe, check the micro-tag on that, please."

She sighed dramatically but did as I asked. At least she seemed in a better mood, even if cheering her had left my stomach roiling. "It says AF-120."

I checked the mine map on my wristlet. We were right on course. "Good. Let's keep walking."

After that, no one said anything for a while. I watched my footsteps. Watched the edges of our helmet lights where the rock changed from bright, reddish-brown to cool, dark shadows. Zoe's words about the IC repeated in my head. They'd probably heard about the sabotage by now. If the *Platinum Phoenix* hadn't contacted them directly, well, Zoe had posted pictures on the internet.

My stomach clenched into a fist of dread. She shouldn't have uploaded those. I imagined the IC ripping the *Platinum Phoenix* apart, destroying everyone's work on everything from aeroponics to magnetohydrodynamics.

I wanted to go to Earth. But I didn't want to go like this.

I KEPT track of our progress on the map. We weren't moving as fast as I'd thought we would. I wished we'd already hiked the narrow gallery, gotten across whatever that strange line was, and were standing at the shaft. Walking in the lower-g pulled on different muscles in my legs, leaving me feeling tugged sideways and wrung out. Slouching kept my head from hitting the ceiling, but it made my airpack seem heavier.

We'd be lucky to reach the shaft in two hours.

Zoe mumbled another number, and I checked my wristlet map. Then we kept going. No one asked how far we'd come. Maybe they were too tired to notice our slow pace.

I was tired.

Despite the heat-regulating system in my suit, the coldness of the mines soaked into me. Why would one of my classmates risk this dark vacuum to slice up a shifter? That thought turned, sluggish in my mind. I was missing something. Something important.

A kid couldn't have done this alone. They'd need at least one tech to suit them up, make sure the cage ran smoothly, and keep the mining equipment from crushing them. This wasn't an individual doing something rash on a whim. It was a team.

More than one person on the asteroid was willing to risk my life, Zoe's, and Cornelius'. Did they do it to hurt us? Did they think it was funny? Who wanted the *Platinum Phoenix* to fail?

Zoe rattled another number. I checked it. Cornelius lagged. We all struggled with the lower gravity. My skin was slick with perspiration inside my suit, making the oxygen in my helmet taste as stale as two-day-old socks. I tried to ignore the sweat trickling down my neck that I couldn't wipe away. What I wouldn't give for a drink of water.

By the time we reached the next pillar, Cornelius' panting buzzed through my helmet speaker.

"It's time for a break," I said. "Everyone sit down. We'll start again in a bit. Zoe, what's the number?"

She slumped next to me. "Let me catch my breath first."

Cornelius leaned his helmet against the pillar and wheezed. The broken rock floor was even less comfortable than aluminum chairs. By now, rust-red dust covered us—like we were already dead things of the past and just didn't realize it yet.

I sucked on my tongue, trying to get some moisture back. More than ever, I missed the long-comm. I needed a calm voice to listen to instead of trying to be that voice for my crew. This hike would be so much easier with a tech in my ear telling me we were going to make it.

Except, one of those techs had helped cause this. I paused. My dad had said the computers around ore-intake crashed last night. Data lost. That couldn't have been an accident. Someone was covering their tracks—a tech and a kid, at least. Everyone older than me was too big. I doubted anyone younger than Cornelius would dare do it.

"All right," Zoe said, interrupting my thoughts. "We're at AK-210."

Which adults would willingly endanger kids? Who had a reason to? And which adult could get one of my classmates to do it?

I'd always been proud that my dad was a well-liked teacher, but now it gnawed at me. It couldn't be him, though. He didn't want me—or anyone else—up here.

"Uh, Ana, you still there?" Zoe asked.

"Right. Tell me the number again."

"AK-210," Zoe repeated, exhaustion dulling her voice.

I tapped my wristlet, prompting it to project the mine map

across my sleeve. I breathed slowly and tried to act normal as I scanned the image. Then I double-checked it. My throat hardened into a lump, and all the hot sweat slicking my body turned cold.

We were lost.

CHAPTER 18

Was this pillar mistagged, or had Zoe read a number wrong? Maybe I'd checked one of them incorrectly? If the number was right, we'd drifted a half-kilometer off course to the left. The mine map glared across my arm.

"What's wrong?" Cornelius asked. Undistracted by video games, he seemed to know when I was upset.

Everything. I didn't know where we were. One kid and some number of adults had sabotaged the shifter. We could have been safe if I hadn't been so stubborn and insisted on finishing the repairs. If the IC took me to Mendel, they'd take Cornelius away from our parents, too.

Cornelius kept peering at me.

"Just...correcting our course," I said.

"What!" Zoe jerked upright. "You said—you said this would be easy!"

"I said it was better than sitting and doing nothing!" I snapped. "Nothing in space is easy!"

Zoe shut up.

I exhaled. Zoe and Cornelius—they could flip out. I needed to be their calm. But I couldn't think of a single reassuring thing to say to Zoe.

I craved the sound of my mother's voice, reading something. Anything. Before the fab broke, if Cornelius or I got sick, she'd slip away from the refineries to read stories to us in the hospital.

My wristlet could read books, but it always read them perfectly. It was comforting to hear the stumbles. To know she was there, next to me.

"How...did this happen?" Cornelius asked.

For a moment, I thought he meant one of our classmates betraying us. But I hadn't mentioned that out loud. "Either this pillar's mislabeled, or we misread the last several pillars."

"Oh." Such a small, scared sound. He looked down. The light from his headlamp pooled around us, golden and brilliant. A tiny haven from the darkness of stone and vacuum. "Which one of you messed up this time?"

"Me," I blurted, "because I'm the leader. Keeping track of everything is my responsibility." We were bickering enough without worrying who to blame.

Zoe hugged her legs to her chest. "No, it's my fault," she whispered, her voice hoarse like she might cry. So much for cheering her up earlier.

"It's not. In fact, given my failures, I think I should apologize by splitting my pay for this mission between you and Cornelius, all zero creds of it," I joked in my brightest voice.

It was like she didn't even hear me. "*I dropped the long-comm.* If we hadn't lost that...you would've repaired the shifter right. Or at least we'd be able to tell the techs what went wrong, and then they'd tell us what to do. Even if we still had to hike to the other shaft, they could have tracked us and kept us on course. Why did I even come up here?"

"Because you're brave. Because the *Platinum Phoenix* needed you."

Zoe shook her head, so I kept talking. "Zoe, don't be hard on yourself. Dropping the long-comm was an accident, just like the shifter malfunctioning."

The difference was, I could have chosen not to fix it. I could have remembered my father's warning and respected the dangers of space. I could have ordered us all down the shaft while we still had that choice.

Zoe sniffled.

This conversation wasn't helping. We needed something else to focus on—like not tripping in this lower-g. I checked the map. "We'll go straight until we reach the mine wall, then follow it to the narrow gallery. It'll lead us right to the other shaft. No problems. Just a little extra walking. Let's get moving."

Given that I didn't want anyone to burn out, I set a slow pace. Zoe tried to wipe her nose, but her gloved hand hit the front of her helmet. She'd have that snot on her face until we managed to get back home.

I made a mental note not to cry.

As we walked, I glanced at my wristlet. We'd been using our airpacks for over three hours—less than five hours left. Surely, we'd be home and safe long before that.

Our helmets only lit strips of the rust-colored floor and low ceiling. Everything else was darkness as we shuffled in a straight line, hoping for the next pillar to appear. That uncanny silence rang in my ears.

Down in the colony, were my parents settling in for bed? Was everyone running about, trying to figure out what to do? I wondered if our classmates knew. Maybe the older ones. Would they tell the little kids?

Which one of my classmates had come up here last night and snipped all those wires? And who had helped them?

We reached the next pillar. "Zoe, what's the number?"

"AK-220."

I tapped my wristlet and checked the map. The pillars hadn't been mislabeled—we'd drifted. I had no way to know if I'd misheard Zoe, if she'd misspoken, or both. I enjoyed human error when my mother was reading to me—navigating the mines was another matter. I chewed my lip, but that made my stomach growl. What I wouldn't do for some water to soothe my freeze-dried mouth.

"AK-220," I parroted back. "That's correct?"

"Yes."

We wouldn't make another navigation mistake. "We'll reach the gallery fine—just a bit slower than planned." I stretched my cramping calves. I needed to think about my team, not the people who'd put our lives in peril. "Everyone holding up? Zoe?"

"I'm good." She shrugged.

"Cornelius?"

"I want to go home," he whimpered.

I squeezed his shoulder and tried to make my voice sound brave. "I'll get us there."

I gave them a tooth-hurting grin that didn't match my fears. But I got two half-hearted smiles in return. We kept marching.

My mind drifted to Jayden, trembling so bad she threw up. If she'd been up here last night, that would explain her nervousness. But I couldn't think of a single reason why she'd do it.

Dae-sung had congratulated me on getting a mission. But I couldn't imagine him cutting those wires just to make me happy.

My stomach writhed. I hoped neither of them had done this, but *someone* had.

I tried to think through the techs—Lily, Daniel, Clarke, Choi, Robinson, Myung—plus a dozen more. Any of them could have helped plan this. Heck, all of them could have planned it together.

Mom. My heart stopped cold. She had the skills to pull off sabotage. She might have been the first person to notice the computer failures, too. I wasn't sure. But she hated me going on these missions as much as Dad. She'd been home last night. All night. Hadn't she?

Besides, if she'd planned this, wouldn't she have asked me to cut the wires?

None of the techs I knew had spoken up at the hearing. Governor Cardoso, CEO Yun, and Nurse Hwang had been for the mission. Nurse Oliveira and Dr. Kim were against it. Plus others, but I couldn't remember them all. Even if I could, that didn't help me narrow it down. I wasn't sure if the saboteurs wanted to be discovered or not. Our mission hadn't been a sure thing.

"Ana? What's wrong?" Cornelius asked again.

"Nothing."

"But your face is all wrinkled like you're thinking too hard."

I put on an even bigger smile—one hundred percent fake. "It's nothing."

"We're lost again, aren't we?" He dropped his voice as if that would stop his audio from streaming into Zoe's helmet.

She halted. "We're lost?"

Darkness swallowed the edges of our headlamps. We still couldn't see a pillar in any direction.

"We are not lost!"

Zoe tossed her arms up. "I don't want you pretending to make me feel better! I want to know. I'm stuck up here, too."

"Nothing's wrong!"

Zoe glared, but Cornelius was worse. His brown eyes rounded with pity and concern that begged me to tell him.

"I..." I couldn't form the sour words in my mouth—that one of our classmates had done this to us. And probably someone in our Tuesday workshop group at that. "I really have to pee, okay?"

Zoe blinked.

"I know they suited us up in the 'absorbent underwear,' but

I've never used mine, and I don't know if it'll chafe afterward," I said. "So stop flipping out about the funny faces."

Cornelius shrugged. "Mine doesn't rub funny at all."

Details I didn't want to know. Zoe stepped back from him.

After not too much longer, we reached the next pillar. The number on it checked out. We were on course. Good. "Let's take another break. A short one."

I sat against the pillar, facing the direction we were headed.

Cornelius joined me and tapped his wristlet. He pulled up an old game we used to play together years ago—a cheesy thing with too-bright graphics called *Penguin Mountain*.

"Want to play? You can be the green penguin."

"Maybe in a minute."

I watched him, wristlet light flickering over his bumpy sleeve as he used a finger to navigate an orange, tobogganing penguin down a mountain cluttered with rocks, seals, and cliffs. He leaned back against the pillar, a soft smile spreading over his face. "Do you remember how we used to play this together? All the time? Before you became obsessed with biology and Mendel?"

Obsessed seemed a bit strong. "Yeah, you said the penguins were all siblings and gave them the last name of Friend. Marcia Friend, Bartholomew Friend..." I struggled to remember the other four.

"Yeah, they were family, so they were friends forever. It seemed like a good name."

A super cheesy name. I sighed. "Cornelius, how can you relax enough to play video games right now?"

He shrugged, making the orange penguin stumble. Juan Friend? João Friend? It had been too long. "You're here. And we're not lost. We'll be okay, right?"

He had too much faith in me. But I patted his shoulder anyway. "That's right. We'll be fine."

Zoe snorted. "Three kids, trapped in an asteroid mine—that's fine? With a disaster like this, my photos are probably going viral, and I can't even enjoy it."

I almost liked it better when she moped. Trying to be a good friend, I said, "Don't worry, your website will be waiting for you when we get back."

"Yeah, or we'll be corpses for the rest of *ever*. All the other kids will get a free ride to Earth from the IC. We'll pay the price for their freedom."

Cornelius scowled at her. "Stop saying that!"

His penguin crashed into a rock and respawned at the top of the mountain, but he didn't notice.

"Stop what?" Zoe asked.

"We're not going to die, and the IC's not tearing my family apart. I won't go."

Zoe laughed, then said what I'd been thinking. "I'm sure the officers will listen real nice when you tell them that, then drag you off anyway. No one cares about what kids want."

"You're making that up!" Cornelius' voice frizzed in my speaker.

I felt like I was trapped in an ore crusher with Zoe on one side and Cornelius on the other. "Hey," I said, "let's all take a deep breath and—"

"You really think the IC will ignore this? Sabotage. Child endangerment. We're all getting off this rock, Corny, whether you like it or not. If I were you, I'd be doing a victory dance. If we live to see it, that is."

"I didn't come up here to lose my family."

My stomach squirmed. Why *had* Cornelius come up here? He'd been acting so strange—flipping between terrified and cheerful. "I never did ask you why you volunteered for this mission."

Cornelius winced and looked away, mumbling under his

breath. Embarrassed? Guilty? Was it possible that *Cornelius* had sabotaged the shifter?

I couldn't imagine what he'd gain from it. "What were you going to spend your pay on?" I asked.

"Hadn't thought about it," he muttered, shoulders slumped miserably. "But I don't want to go home if the IC is going to take me away from my family."

Cornelius hadn't thought his statement through. We needed to make it home soon, or the results would be a lot worse than an IC investigation. I checked the time on my wristlet. 2304 hours. We'd stepped out of decompression three and a half hours ago. We had about four and a half hours of oxygen left—probably less, given all our physical activity.

"You should thank the IC for rescuing you from this prison," Zoe said. "You didn't ask to live here."

"I didn't ask to live on Earth either," Cornelius snapped. "How is having the IC decide stuff for me better than my parents picking where we live? At least here, I'm with them."

Zoe laughed. "Maybe you don't care right now, but once you get to Earth, you'll see there's a lot more to life than video games."

"You think I'm dumb, don't you?" he asked Zoe, but then he glanced at me.

I winced. During dinner, I'd sounded just like Zoe. I'd been mad. And worried. Apparently, the worry was justified. "Cornelius..."

I thought it was dumb that he volunteered. That wasn't the same as thinking *he* was dumb.

"I'm not stupid," Cornelius hugged his arms to his chest. "I'm up here, the same as you."

Again, I wished that he was back home. It would have been nice to know that if I died, the rest of my family could grieve together. Instead, my parents would be all alone.

Zoe laughed. "Corny, I'm sure you'll grow out of being an idiot, but, I mean, really. You've never done IDPOP. You play video games instead of doing something valuable with your time—like reading the news or pursuing botany or photography. You're up in the mines—big deal. You can't even handle a socket wrench with those gloves on. Worst of all, you actually think the *Platinum Phoenix* is a nice place to live."

My marrow chilled from the base of my neck to my toes. Zoe hated the *Platinum Phoenix*.

Cornelius couldn't be the saboteur. Neither could Jayden or Dae-sung. None of them were good enough with those tiny, star-shaped screws I'd found scattered around the shifter. They would have needed a pry bar or a laser cutter to get that panel off.

Zoe fit in the cage. She'd skipped IDPOP this afternoon because she was exhausted. Only Zoe and I were any good with the star-shaped screws. And I hadn't done it.

Cornelius' confidence disappeared. He stared at me with big eyes, as if I'd said all those hurtful things, not Zoe. I tried to mimic my father's best stern-teacher voice. "Zoe, you can't talk to my brother that way."

Cornelius beamed.

"Ana, he—"

"Stop!" I wanted to confront her right here and ask if she'd cut the wires. Had she posted pics to her website and dropped the long-comm on purpose to get the IC involved? She'd been unruffled by the cut wires and unconcerned about losing the long-comm. Then she'd freaked out about being trapped up here.

But I couldn't accuse her without Cornelius overhearing. And I didn't know how he'd handle that. He'd been reacting strangely to everything today too, and we still had at least an hour—if everything went well—before we got to the shaft.

"It's time to start walking again. Zoe, you take the front for now. I'll take the rear."

She wrinkled her nose but did as I'd ordered. I watched her every step.

I didn't want to give her a chance to do anything else to hurt me—or Cornelius.

CHAPTER 19

Zoe's white helmet bobbed just below the ragged ceiling as we trudged along. Was I jumping to conclusions about her? Did I want to make up an answer so the darkness wouldn't seem so real? I was pretty sure she was the only other person who could have done this.

"Zoe, do you really hate living on the asteroid?" I asked.

"Who wouldn't right now?" she tapped the ceiling with her fist. Red dust drifted over her.

"I still like it," Cornelius said.

Zoe audibly mumbled, "Because you're an idiot."

"My family's here," he stated, as if that were the only thing that mattered.

At least with us walking single-file, Cornelius couldn't see my concerned face. He didn't ask me what was wrong. And I didn't have to lie to him.

We reached the wall—a reddish-black curtain of stone. Keeping it on our left, we continued until we reached the gallery.

Thanks to the scrubbers, we had a flat floor, but the walls were rough and lumpy. Humans didn't build hallways like this. Not for themselves.

I peered down it, but our lights didn't reach far. Three beams faded away into pitch blackness.

"Go ahead, Zoe," I said.

She glared at me. "You want the rear because you're too scared to lead!"

I bristled. Of course I was scared! Anyone would be! But in some ways, I feared her more than the mines. These tunnels in the asteroid weren't malicious or spiteful—they just *were*. How could Zoe want the *Platinum Phoenix* to fail? How could she play with the dangers of space, risking my life and my brother's in the process?

I'd thought we were friends. Best friends.

"You'd rather be in the back, where you couldn't see if anything sneaks up on us?" I asked. "I'm happy to go first if you want to—"

"I'm going," she snapped and strode into the gallery.

Cornelius looked over his shoulder at me, eyes wide. "You think there's something—"

"Don't worry about it. I'm sure we're fine. The mines are empty. It's just the three of us."

Just us and a saboteur, but I was nearly certain that still made three people. My mouth tasted like chalk and my head hurt. I didn't know who had helped Zoe. I didn't know if it was their idea or hers. But if someone had asked me? Told me that all I needed to do for a ticket to Earth was slash some wires, post some pictures, and drop a long-comm...would I have done it?

I wanted to think I knew the answer. I wanted to believe I'd say no and report the culprits to Governor Cardoso, my parents, or Dr. Fletcher.

But half of me still hoped I'd get thrown into the IC's protective custody. That at the end of this, even though I didn't have a paycheck, I'd still have a ticket to Earth.

ACCORDING to my wristlet watch and the map, we were covering ground faster than before. We didn't have to worry about getting lost—there was nowhere to get turned around in this one, long hall. But the scenery never changed. Every step forward revealed more rock nearly identical to what we'd just passed.

"This is like Helio Gracie and Valdemar Santana," Cornelius said.

"Who?" I asked.

"Helio Gracie, inventor of Brazilian Jiu-Jitsu. He fought Valdemar Santana—a much bigger guy—in an almost *four-hour* match. On and on and on and..."

"I get it," I mumbled, the gallery stretching, never-ending, before us. Little piles of dust and rubble gathered in the corners.

"So who won?" Zoe asked. "The little guy, or the big one?" She gestured at the red rock all around us. We definitely weren't the heavyweight here.

Cornelius coughed. "Well, Santana. But Gracie did fight for a crazy-long time."

How cheerful. "How do you even know about all of that?"

"*Martial Battle* 3000X. It's supposed to be one of the best video games ever made, but Mom won't let me buy it. I've read all about it, though. You can play as Helio Gracie."

We walked in silence for a moment—everyone's tired breathing buzzing in my speakers. Our footsteps remained eerily soundless in the vacuum of the mines.

Cornelius chirped up again. "Hey, Ana. Did Mom ever read you that Greek story about the Minotaur's labyrinth?"

"Yeah. Thanks, Cornelius."

I don't know if Cornelius didn't catch my tone or if his helmet malfunctioned and he hadn't heard me. "I was thinking about the part where the prisoners could walk around for days and days and days and never find their way out."

"Idiot," Zoe said, not breaking stride. "We don't have days and days. Do you know what happens if our air runs out?"

I sighed. "Zoe, leave him alone. Can't we—"

"The air keeps pressure in our helmets. Before you can suffocate, your helmet will depressurize, and your head will turn to jelly." She paused to glance behind at Cornelius, but he seemed unaffected.

"Can we say it's marmalade? I miss marmalade, especially the little bits of kumquat peel," he said. Aeroponics grew them before the water shortage.

"Cornelius...you wouldn't get to eat... It was a metaphor," I stumbled. "And a bad one. Our exhaled carbon dioxide would keep us pressurized. We'd die from CO_2 poisoning."

"I'm hungry," Cornelius said. "I liked Zoe's food metaphor better."

Zoe turned and made a disgusted face at him.

I checked my wristlet. 0030 hours. Three hours past when I usually went to bed. Five hours up here. Three hours of oxygen left. And maybe one or two kilometers to go. My muscles ached all over, like the suit was crushing me instead of keeping me alive.

"Did you ever read the Korean fairy tale with the three princesses?" Cornelius asked. "The one where they're all trapped in the land below the earth? By an evil ogre? I bet they had taller ceilings than us because ogres are super tall."

I did not need to start thinking about ogres. "Cornelius, could you go back to talking about video games?"

"Oooh! I watched a demo of a new *Lord of the Rings* game. There's a level for the Mines of Moria."

"Could you pick something *happy?*"

"The Mines of Moria aren't so bad. Everyone lives."

"Yeah," Zoe said, "except *Gandalf.*"

"He comes back!" Cornelius replied.

Somehow, if our air ran out, I didn't think any of us would get a magical resurrection.

Zoe stopped cold.

I sighed. I just wanted to walk in pain and quiet. "What now?"

Zoe's voice quivered. "This...this shouldn't be here."

I stepped up next to her. The gallery had opened up—we'd finally reached the end of it. But, not ten meters away, a long V-shaped gorge cut across the floor. I turned my head, sweeping my light back and forth across it. One end undercut the wall on our right with no way across. The other side continued out into the ever-present darkness.

I tapped the map up. Now I knew what that odd squiggly line was. My throat tightened as if already struggling for air.

"Can we go around it?" Zoe asked.

I stared at the map. The gorge extended from this wall of the mine in a wide, wiggly arch. The shaft was only a quarter kilometer away, just past the chasm. To go around... I asked my wristlet to calculate it.

Three kilometers of walking. My aching legs quivered as I stared at the map.

"Ana?" Cornelius asked, not disturbed in the least. "Which way do we go?"

I didn't know. "Let's take a good look at it before we make any decisions."

The three of us walked together, side by side, and peered over the edge.

The fissure looked natural—as jagged as shattered obsidian, with nothing to erode and soften the edges of the rock. Had it always been here? Or had this pocket ripped open when engineers spun the asteroid to create our artificial gravity?

The gorge almost looked like some prehistoric creature, with spikes jutting into the air and gills slashed across its surface. Bits of dark ice glittered in its teeth.

Some mining rubble dusted the ground around my feet. I tossed a pebble in and watched it fall, trying to gauge the distance. It wasn't that deep—maybe eight meters. There seemed to be plenty of ledges and hand-holds everywhere.

"So, crew leader," Cornelius said brightly, "do we go down or hike around it?"

I didn't know what we should do. What if I picked the wrong thing? I didn't want to decide—I didn't want to be in charge anymore.

"We know where we are right now," Zoe said. "I'd rather roll down this and scrape our way back up than wander anymore."

"I don't think we'd get lost. We'd follow the gorge," I said, tracing the wristlet-projected map on my sleeve.

Zoe leaned over me, peering at the map. "How far did we walk to come here?"

"Almost five kilometers."

"How much farther would we have to walk to get around?" she asked.

"Three."

"Yeah, I'd say that makes our chances of getting lost pretty high."

I wasn't worried about getting lost, but her words made me pause. It had taken us three hours to travel five kilometers. We'd need almost forty-five minutes to get all three of us down the shaft and ten or fifteen minutes more to take a mine cart back to the colony. That gave us less than two hours in the mines.

We'd walked that far in an hour in the straightforward gallery. But wouldn't we keep getting slower? My legs throbbed with exhaustion, and my airpack straps dug into my shoulders. We didn't have any water. How many breaks would we need to march another three kilometers? With how heavily we'd been breathing, I doubted we actually had two hours left. What if it was only one?

Cornelius shrugged. "The gorge doesn't look that bad. It's kinda like *Penguin Mountain*, but with less snow."

Zoe and Cornelius both watched me, waiting.

I didn't want to fight them. Running out of oxygen would kill us. Climbing the gorge was still up for debate. "I'll go down first, then."

"Good luck." Zoe didn't even sound sarcastic.

I exhaled, turned, and put my foot down onto the first ledge. I was the oldest and the strongest. If anyone else fell on the descent, I'd be the one who got hit. If anyone needed a hand up on the other side, I'd be the one to pull.

Even though it meant I couldn't keep an eye on Zoe.

"Cornelius, you come next, then Zoe." I wanted him close to me.

I shifted to my right, finding the next gash across the rock. Climbing down the first six meters wasn't so bad, really. I tried to tell myself that the gym inside the *Platinum Phoenix* had gotten a hyper-realistic upgrade. Dae-sung would have loved this.

Then my foot slipped on a patch of ice. I shrieked and threw myself against the wall.

The stone scraped my breastbone hard, but I stopped skidding after a meter. Once I got my feet firmly planted on a curved ledge, I felt the front of my suit—no tears. I exhaled.

"Careful as you come down," I said. "There's ice and mining rubble and—"

A scream filled my helmet. Something hit my elbow.

It took me another heartbeat to realize the two things were related. Cornelius had fallen to the bottom of the fissure.

CHAPTER 20

I scrambled down, whacking my knee. The helmet speaker transmitted his every cry and groan into my ears.

"Cornelius, I'm coming. Hold still."

I skidded the last meter to him. He lay on his back, sobbing. I reached to take his pulse, forgetting that I couldn't—not through the suit. If we still had the long-comm, the techs would have his vitals. They could have told me if his pulse was weak and rapid, a sign of shock.

The only thing I had to go on was his zombie-ashen face.

"What hurts?" I asked. I didn't want to move him without figuring out where he was injured.

"Arm."

His right arm lay limp at his side, but with the thick pressure suit around it, I couldn't see anything wrong. Thankfully, his sleeve only showed scuffs and a few frayed threads.

"Can you move your arm?" I asked.

He tried. And he screamed.

"Okay. Let's not do that again." The sound of my pulse pounded in my ears. I thought through the report I'd made for my dad. First-aid. Shock. Elevate the legs to get blood to the brain. I pulled his feet onto my lap.

I looked up at the fissure wall in front of me. Not so long ago, that had seemed a short distance—an easy climb.

"He looks bad," Zoe said. Her hand touched my shoulder.

I jumped. I hadn't realized she'd climbed down; I couldn't hear her footfalls.

Zoe had been standing behind Cornelius. Did she push him? A fall could have killed him. Could have punctured the cells in his airpack or torn his pressure suit wide open.

I clenched my jaw, watching her stare at Cornelius. Was she faking her concerned, wrinkled frown?

"Cornelius," I said, hard and cold. "How'd this happen?"

"I...I fell. Slipped," he whimpered. "I'm...sorry, I..."

He thought I was mad at him. I softened my voice. "It's okay. Cornelius, you just focus on breathing. Zoe, go up first."

"Me?" She turned and blinked.

"I'm going to help Cornelius. I need you at the top to give us a hand up."

And so I could see everything she was doing.

Zoe nodded, then climbed. Pulling on Cornelius' good arm and pushing on his back, I got him standing. "Are you dizzy?"

He shrugged one shoulder, his breathing too labored to talk. I pursed my lips. I couldn't exactly bring a doctor to him; I had to get him out of the mines. How to haul him up? I couldn't carry him on my shoulders. None of the first aid lifts I'd studied covered cliffs. I glanced up, watching Zoe scale the rocks, agile as a spider.

"You're going to have to do this with one arm. But I'll be right behind you."

Cornelius nodded. He got his good hand in a groove and pulled himself onto a narrow ledge, his big boots splayed. But he couldn't let go to grab the next handhold without losing his balance.

I became his balance, pressing the small of his back forward. "I've got you. Let go and grab the next one."

Cornelius grunted and lunged for it. He needed help for the next step, too. I stood with my feet shoulder-width apart, braced my knees, and then spotted him as he reached for another handhold.

We did another step. And another. Cornelius wept as we went. My forearms burned, and my palms went clammy inside their gloves.

"Are you guys sure this will work?" Zoe asked.

I glanced up. She peered at us from the rim.

"I'm getting him to the top."

I positioned myself to help him with the next ledge.

"We could leave him at the bottom," Zoe said. "The two of us could go to the shaft. You could come back with some rope and haul him up. Might be easier."

I wasn't going to leave my little brother, alone and injured in the dark, at the bottom of a fissure in hard vacuum. "No."

"Th-thanks," Cornelius managed, teeth chattering. He tried to turn to face me and lost his grip.

I widened my stance, dug in my heels, and braced my arms forward. I held most of his weight.

"Move!" I snapped, my arms shaking, ready to give out.

Cornelius grunted in pain as he lunged for a new handhold.

Exhaustion blazed from my shoulder blades to my fingertips, but we made it another step. And another. And another.

At the top, Zoe grabbed Cornelius' good hand and yanked him up and over the lip of the fissure. He banged his bad arm against the rock. I only heard the first part of his scream; my overloaded helmet speaker frizzed the rest. Had Zoe hurt him on purpose?

I glared, but I didn't have the energy to climb after him any faster. Zoe didn't attack Cornelius, though. She extended a hand down and pulled me up, too.

I panted, sweat dripping into my eyes, but I couldn't wipe it away. My arms hung as limp as Cornelius'.

My brother collapsed onto the floor. He used his good arm like a pillow and flopped the injured one on top of his chest.

"It's no time for a nap," Zoe urged. "We'll help you walk if you need it."

I plopped next to him, once again pulling his feet up onto my lap to elevate them. "I could use a break too."

"We're...we're so close!" Panic edged her voice.

"He's injured. Let him rest for five minutes," I said, not adding that my arms felt as functional as a mylar rag doll's.

Zoe paced for a moment but eventually sat. "This is a waste of time. I'm so tired of being up here."

"We'll all be home soon." I glanced at Cornelius. His eyes were closed. I lowered my voice. "Cornelius?"

"Mm lemme rest," he muttered.

His breathing seemed more regular, his face less pale. Maybe he wasn't in shock anymore? Anyone would be exhausted after trekking through the mines, after all, and Cornelius had never been good at staying up past his bedtime in the first place.

"Cornelius?" I whispered even softer, but he didn't respond. His breathing was smooth and deep. Poor Cornelius. I'd have to wake him up in a few minutes—as soon as I could move my arms again.

Zoe glowered. "I can't believe we're just sitting here with the shaft so close."

Bile and anger filled my throat. Cornelius could have died— we all could have died—and she'd endangered us on purpose. I couldn't keep the words back anymore. "I can't believe *you* sabotaged the shifter."

Zoe jerked back, eyes wide. "I...how... I mean, I didn't..." She trailed off, lips pursed.

Cornelius didn't so much as stir. He was fast asleep.

"Why?" I demanded, my whisper harsh.

She wrinkled her nose. "Can't you figure that one out? If you were me, you would have done the same thing. I can't stay on this rock for another two years, Ana. If we get the IC's attention, all the kids can come to Earth. Not just you."

I didn't like that anyone was stuck here. But sabotaging the shifter?

"You won't tell anyone, will you?" Zoe asked, voice softening.

My chest quavered. I didn't know. I traced the pictures of the Mendel Academy in my mind. The wooden desks. The smiling students. The carefree green lawns. If I said nothing, the IC would probably sweep in with an investigation and take me to Earth. But they'd also rip apart every other family—whether or not the kids wanted to leave. I couldn't preserve the *Platinum Phoenix* and make it to Mendel. I'd have to choose.

Zoe had already made her choice.

"Did you...did you arrange for the shifter to cover the shaft?" I asked.

Zoe shook her head, swinging her light wildly from side to side. "I was supposed to take the pictures, then drop the long-comm. A small disaster. Just enough to make sure the IC got involved. You...you didn't cover the shaft on purpose either?"

"Of course not!" I spat, almost forgetting to remain quiet. But Cornelius kept breathing deeply.

Zoe sighed. "I was afraid...afraid that she'd talked to both of us. Me to drop the long-comm, you to seal us in. It makes a bigger story."

"Who talked to you? Who helped you do this?" I demanded.

Zoe gave me a lopsided grin. "No way the IC isn't going to crack down on us now. Ready to go to Earth?"

I hated that she was smiling. Would I have cut those wires if I were in Zoe's place? Risked my friends' lives for it?

I'd been willing to risk my own safety to earn a paycheck—pay I wouldn't get for this failed mission.

"You really think this rock is a prison?" I asked.

"There are only six hundred people here! On Earth, I could *pick* my friends. I could meet all kinds of people."

I peered at her. She'd done this to me—to my little brother and me—for people she didn't even know? "I thought we were friends."

Zoe sighed. "We are, Ana. We are. But...this place is a death trap. Look, it's never going to make money again. It's supposed to transport people to Mars, and no one wants to go there anymore. Everything broke this orbit because we didn't have enough money for supplies. Maybe we'll patch things up this time around. But what happens when we can't fix anything anymore?"

She had a point, and it sounded unnervingly familiar.

"All the adults gave up Earth to come here. Most of those still here—including my parents—wouldn't leave even if they could," Zoe continued. "But we can get all the kids out now, through the IC. None of us chose to be on this sinking ship. Sabotaging the shifter was the only way to get us a lifeboat."

Lifeboat. I'd heard that archaic word on someone else's mouth this morning: *You deserve a lifeboat out of here.*

My stomach felt like I'd swallowed a gallon of ice. "Dr. Fletcher planned this, didn't she?"

CHAPTER 21

Zoe shut up fast. That's how I knew I was right. Dr. Fletcher, Zoe, and at least one tech. Maybe Lily Mason? She didn't have kids, but she cared about us—she'd come up with the idea of making mylar clothes, after all. Maybe that concern had turned into sabotage.

How could Dr. Fletcher risk my life without asking me? She'd been so upset that kids didn't have a choice about living here or not. But she didn't actually want to give us choices. She felt sure our parents were wrong, and now she would force us all to leave.

A tiny part of me felt slighted too. Why had Dr. Fletcher trusted Zoe instead of me? Did she think I wasn't brave enough, wasn't smart enough?

I chewed my lip. If Dr. Fletcher had asked me to be her saboteur...would I have said no? "Who else?" I asked. "Which techs were involved?"

"You can't tell anyone," Zoe repeated. She fidgeted, her fingers making circles around the knees of her suit. "We have to get to Earth. You won't say anything, will you? I'm not a criminal. You don't want to get me arrested."

Right now, the only thing I wanted was to get everyone safely home.

"You *deserve* to be arrested and locked up. You and Dr. Fletcher." But should I tell everyone? Would that stop the IC from coming? Did I want to stop them?

"You can't!"

"I can. I just don't know if I *will*. It's time to go." I couldn't think straight anymore. I wanted to be home where I was safe, where I could breathe in a room full of air. And I needed to talk to someone—but not Dr. Fletcher.

Zoe clenched and unclenched her fists. Her voice shook. "You can't say anything. You'll just make yourself look stupid."

I didn't have the energy to keep arguing with her. "Let's get moving."

I stood. The rocks around us seemed dim, blurry. I tried to blink it away.

Odd. The rocks didn't become any clearer. Maybe I'd bumped my light setting in the fissure. I tried to turn it up.

I'd forgotten I'd left it on maximum for so long—ever since I started splicing those wires. The light wasn't malfunctioning. Its charge was nearly dead. No amount of fiddling made it any brighter. I swallowed, but my throat still felt like sand.

"Cornelius. Cornelius." I bent over and rubbed his chest. His eyes opened to half-slits. "Time to go."

He jerked away from me, then stumbled to his feet. No smiles. He didn't wait for me or Zoe to take the lead; moaning in pain, he shuffled toward the shaft.

I sighed. It was 0103 now, Cornelius had been hiking the mines for hours, and he had a broken arm. I couldn't expect a good mood.

And I had no good mood of my own to share. I trudged behind Cornelius. At least if Zoe lashed out at one of us, it would be me.

We followed the mine wall—no way to get lost. I couldn't hear our feet, just Cornelius' wheezing breath. Still, the floor seemed to stretch forever.

My arms hung like dead weight. I missed 1g, normal traction, and knees that didn't scream every time I moved.

Cornelius' light caught the cage first—shimmering, waiting for us, like a metallic phoenix offering new life. Pride and relief flooded me. *We'd made it.*

"Cornelius, I want you to go first."

"Trying to get rid of me. Again," he mumbled, not turning around, not moving. "You've always chosen that academy over staying with your family."

I frowned. It wasn't like him to be this surly. "You're injured —you should go down first. Get in."

He jerked away. "You just hate me."

Something wasn't right. I stepped behind him and saw what I hadn't before: his airpack was dented. A handful of tiny holes had pierced some of the air cells. How much air did he still have? Which cells had his suit used first?

He couldn't have much oxygen left if he was becoming delirious.

I remembered not having enough oxygen to breathe. I'd wanted Cornelius to never experience the same thing. Swallowing, I tried to make my voice firm and sure. "Cornelius, you need to get in now."

"No."

"Your air cells are punctured," I said calmly. "You need to get in."

I reached for his good arm, to drag him into the cage if I had to. But he jumped back.

His eyes were wide, wild. "You're both trying to kill me!"

"What? Cornelius, no, I'm—"

"I heard you two talking! I'm not as dumb as you think I am, just because I play video games!" His voice cracked my speakers. "You both think if I die, the IC will take you to Earth, huh? I'm not going to let you murder me!"

And I thought he'd been asleep. "Cornelius, you

misunderstood because you're so tired. No one's trying to kill you."

"You're lying!"

Cornelius sprinted away, faster than I thought he could move. I turned and took two steps to follow, but my dying headlamp illuminated little more than the rock under my feet. Cornelius vanished into the darkness in front of me. "Zoe, come on. We've got to get him."

She didn't answer, so I turned around. Zoe already stood in the cage. She pulled the ramp-door shut and began descending.

"Zoe!"

"Sorry," she said. I could only see the moving cable now, lowering her down that shaft. "I'm not getting arrested."

"W-what?"

Her voice came in through the speakers as clearly as if she were standing next to me. "I know you're going to tell, so I'll talk first. I'll say how *you* did all of this for a chance to earn another paycheck. You can go to jail instead of me. You've been so desperate to get to Earth, they'll believe my story."

"Zoe! Cornelius doesn't *have air*. I *need* your helmet light. Come back up!"

"Good luck, Ana. You're smart. I'm sure you'll both be fine." She said it like she hoped it was true, but her voice wavered.

"ZOE!" I screamed, the speaker's shrill feedback ringing in my ears.

Silence. How could she leave? How could she just *hope* Cornelius would be okay?

My stomach sank. She'd already made these choices once before, sabotaging the shifter and endangering the whole colony.

I could wait by the shaft, follow her right away, and tell the adults what really happened before they had time to let her story sink in. Before they believed her.

In my fading helmet light, I could barely make out the edges of the shaft. The rocks all looked almost blue. Blue and dead, like Cornelius would be if I didn't find him.

I turned away from the shaft and jogged back down the wall. Let Zoe lie. Let them lock me away. I wasn't leaving my brother up here.

CHAPTER 22

"Cornelius?" I called. My voice would carry to his helmet, but he'd have to be conscious to hear me. "Cornelius, I'm coming for you. Zoe already left, but I'm here. I didn't do anything to hurt you."

He grunted. Or was that a sob? I glanced behind me before remembering that was just the direction of my helmet speaker.

"Cornelius, my light is dying. I can't see well."

Was that spark up ahead his helmet lamp, or was I imagining things?

"I'm trying to find you," I pleaded.

"I turned my helmet lamp off," he said. "You won't find me. I won't let you."

"Cornelius, you're not thinking straight. Where are you?"

"Someplace happy."

Happy? Nowhere in these mines was happy. I jogged along the wall, terrified that if I struck out to search somewhere else, I'd get lost. Permanently.

But wouldn't Cornelius try to hide somewhere I couldn't easily find him?

I paused, panting. "Cornelius, I'm coming."

"Go away."

I stepped out from the wall. I tapped my wristlet on, but it didn't give me much more light—just a faint glow over my arm. "I want to find you. You need to get down the shaft. You need to get air. I'm trying to help you, Cornelius. I'm not your enemy; I'm your sister, your friend."

"I'm with my only friends."

Friends? There wasn't anyone else up here.

"Maybe I'm not like you. I don't know what I want to do when I'm grown up. Is that so bad?" he blubbered. "I just knew the people I wanted to be with."

"Cornelius...I'm the only other person in the mines."

He sniffed. "I volunteered for this mission because I wanted to spend time with you. Before you left *forever*."

Those words felt like a stab to the gut. "Cornelius..." I wasn't sure what else to say. "I won't stop being your sister if I go to Earth."

"You'll just stop being my friend. Enjoy the snow there."

Cornelius definitely didn't have enough oxygen to think straight. Porto Alegre almost never got snow.

I bit my lip. *Friend. Snow.* Was he talking about *Penguin Mountain?* I whipped around and sprinted down the wall. He was heading back the way we'd come. The gorge—he'd said that was like the penguin game without snow.

My chest knotted. I hoped I was right. I didn't have time to be wrong.

When I reached the fissure, I turned and ran with it on my left. My poor light didn't illuminate even a meter of it. The gorge loomed like a bottomless pit ready to eat me and my suffocating brother.

I caught a glimmer of light—a real glimmer that grew softer and rounder as I approached.

Cornelius had turned his wristlet on. He couldn't navigate the penguin with his broken arm, so he was clumsily trying to do it with his booted foot.

"Cornelius."

"You won't find me," he mumbled, not realizing I already had.

I ran to him and hugged him as best I could around his airpack and his broken arm. "Cornelius, we need to get you down the shaft."

I wished there was a way to give him some of my oxygen.

He flailed. "I won't let you! I won't let you!"

I tried to pull him up, but he dropped his weight and kicked at my legs. I wasn't strong enough to pick him up, and even if I was, I couldn't carry him.

So, I did the only thing I could think of. I grabbed his broken arm.

Cornelius screamed. I didn't let go. I couldn't. With two hands, I pulled him to his feet. Then, clutching the hand of his injured arm, I hurried back toward the shaft.

My brother scrambled after me, trying to stop me from jolting his arm. "You're hurting me!" he sobbed.

I was sobbing, too, snot running over my upper lip. "I know. But you have to come with me. Will you stop fighting me now?"

"Yes."

I exhaled in relief and moved to his good side to support him with my arm around his shoulder.

Cornelius stomped down on my foot and ran.

I swiped for his broken arm and caught his wrist. He screamed. I wept. But I kept walking, pulling him with me.

I wished I was strong enough to carry him. Or cradle him like a baby.

But I wasn't, so I pulled on his broken arm. Pulled and listened to him howl.

"I'm sorry," I whispered. "I'm sorry."

Making his fracture worse was still better than letting him die.

"You're killing me!" he screamed. "You've never wanted to stay! Earth, Earth, Earth! Put that on my urn!"

Given the low resources on the asteroid, they'd probably put his body through the recycler. But I didn't tell Cornelius that. "I'm here. I didn't abandon you."

"All you want to do is abandon me! A paycheck! A ticket to Earth! Who cares about Cornelius, or Mom, or Dad, or being a family?"

"Cornelius," I begged. "Going to Earth...that wasn't about leaving you behind."

It was about going to something new.

"You're killing me!" he wailed again.

I whispered, "I love you, Cornelius."

I should have played *Penguin Mountain* with him when we stopped at that pillar. I should have noticed why he'd been so strangely happy in the mines—with me. I should have talked to him this morning instead of drooling over the Mendel Academy website one more time.

"I wish I'd stayed behind," he said. "That you and Zoe were trapped up here forever by your horrible selves."

"Cornelius, I'm trying to help you."

And then something far worse than screaming and stomping happened—his voice softened into mumblings I couldn't understand. He didn't fight me when I slipped an arm around him. His eyelids drooped.

Cornelius went limp just as we reached the shaft. The cage had already returned. I yanked the door down.

His chest still rose and fell. He was alive.

I shoved him into the cage, closed the door, then jerked back as the cage descended.

I watched the cables whirl.

Let him live, I prayed. *He's my brother, and I don't want to let him go.*

Now that I couldn't do anything else for him, I felt as wispy as a set of worn-out mylar pants. As the cable descended, taking my brother back to the colony, my helmet light flickered its last rays.

I slumped to the floor in the darkness, in the vacuum, perfectly alone. I listened to the silence. And I waited.

CHAPTER 23

I periodically clicked my wristlet on, using its dim light to check if the cage had returned. I didn't want the wristlet to run out of charge, either.

Tap. Just a hole. Wait. Count to a thousand. Hope Cornelius was still breathing.

Tap. Still a hole. Empty space. Count to a thousand while darkness smothered me, pressed on me—like drowning in a jar of ink. Would Cornelius' last memories be of how much he hated me?

Tap. There stood the cage, shimmering and ethereal in the weak light of my wristlet. Empty and waiting. Someone had taken Cornelius out of there. I hoped that was a good sign. Zoe would have contacted the techs and asked for a mine cart to ride back to the colony as soon as she descended into range of normal comms. Cornelius was probably in the hands of concerned techs and nurses right now.

I crawled in, trusting my hands more than my eyes. I crammed myself flat and pulled the door shut.

The bottom of my stomach fell out from under me as I dropped.

Home. I was headed home. To my mylar clothes. To algae foils. To IDPOP in aeroponics and dinner with my family. Home.

As the cage slowed and the floor pushed against my feet, I

realized that when I thought of home, I didn't picture hills filled with music or wooden desks at an academy.

LILY AND DANIEL waited at the bottom of the shaft, suited up.

"Your parents are eager to see you," Lily said reassuringly. "You're safe now."

They helped me into the mine cart. Either or both of them could have helped Dr. Fletcher with the sabotage. Right then, I didn't care. "Cornelius. How is Cornelius?"

A pause. They shared a look—a *how-much-do-we-tell-her* look.

"Tell me!" I demanded, panic and bile welling in my throat, mixing with all my aches and worries and fears.

"Don't over-exert yourself. You've been through a lot," Daniel said, but he sounded strange. It took me a minute to realize he was talking cautiously, a wobble in his voice. "We got him more oxygen as soon as he was down."

That wasn't an answer—not a real one. "Is Cornelius alive?"

"Yes," Lily finally answered.

Relief washed over me. With it came exhaustion. My eyes closed, and my body crumpled against the side of the mine cart. I felt like I was at double-g, my limbs too heavy to lift. The movement of the minecart thrummed into my bones, soothing and steady.

I wished I could sleep. Sleep until the aches went away. Sleep until I could see Cornelius, talk to him, and see how he was really doing. Sleep until I forgot that my best friend was trying to get me arrested.

But I couldn't sleep. Not at all.

When the cart rolled to a stop, Lily and Daniel spotted me as I climbed out, steadying me twice when my feet slipped. Past the airlock, Nurses Hwang and Oliveira waited for me. They helped me strip off my suit, checking and double-checking my vitals as we went. I asked about Cornelius a dozen times, but they hushed me. Either they didn't know, or they wouldn't tell me.

They dressed me in a clean hospital gown, then put me in a wheelchair. I didn't need a wheelchair, but I didn't protest.

The colony air felt too chill, too crisp—like I'd taken a bite of strawberry sorbet and hit a cold nerve in my teeth.

I'd been to the hospital often enough. We spent the day there instead of at school whenever we had a cold. But today we didn't stop in the room with the bright red rug and cheerful orange beds, made for kids with nothing more serious than a sneeze.

They wheeled me into a private room—a beige cube with too-close walls that wasn't much better than all the red-brown rock I'd spent hours staring at.

Nurse Oliveira gently attached a patch on the inside of my elbow. "This will transmit your vitals to the nurses' station. We'll come running if anything goes wrong. Get some rest, all right?"

She spoke kindly, but that didn't make the heavy metal door thudding shut after her feel less ominous. The thin overhead light gave everything a yellow tinge, like unwashed bed sheets.

Muscles aching in protest, I pushed myself to my feet. Finally, I could go find Cornelius. But when I tried the door, it wouldn't budge.

Locked.

Was I a patient or a prisoner?

EACH TIME I FELL ASLEEP, I jerked awake in a cold sweat. I kept dreaming I was falling through fissures with spikes that tore at me like teeth. Or—worse—that the mines had collapsed on Cornelius, and I couldn't do anything to save him.

I couldn't tell how much time had passed when I woke up and found someone in my room. Not my parents—it was Governor Cardoso. He was watching me.

"I've been waiting for you to wake up."

Obviously. Also, kinda creepy.

Governor Cardoso folded his hands in his lap. "Before we continue, I want you to know this is being recorded."

He flicked his glance towards the ceiling, where a shiny black half-sphere stared down at us.

"Recorded?"

"The IC has claimed jurisdiction and opened a criminal investigation case."

Criminal. Not child protection. "They're not taking all the kids away?"

"Not as of right now. But if you're not helpful and cooperative, they might lash out. I trust you don't want the IC to destroy what's left of the *Platinum Phoenix*?"

My stomach quivered. I didn't want Cornelius and my friends torn away from their homes and families.

"The IC is worried that adults may try to...manipulate your testimony to protect themselves. We know you couldn't have done this on your own. The people you worked with caused a massive crash in the techs' computers to cover their tracks. Your testimony is crucial, Ana."

My throat dried and shriveled. Zoe had done just like she'd threatened. And they *believed* her. "I didn't sabotage the shifter. But I know who did."

Governor Cardoso waited patiently, face unreadable.

"It's Zoe. Zoe and Dr. Fletcher. I'm not sure who else."

A tiny, knowing smile crept into the corner of his mouth. "Ana, you're the only child with a solid motive. Trying to cast blame on your accuser—don't you think that's a little obvious?" he asked.

"I didn't do it!" My face burned. "After I risked my life *twice* for this asteroid, for you and everyone else on it, you don't get to talk to me like I'm stupid!"

He completely ignored everything I'd said, continuing in a calm, business-like voice. "To make sure the people who planned this sabotage can't get to you, only your family and medical personnel will be allowed in this room. At all times, a nurse will monitor your interactions with any visitors." He pointed up at the camera. "It's to prevent any of your accomplices from trying to manipulate or threaten you. It's for your protection."

Protection. As if a nice-sounding word could change the fact that the IC decided my guilt before giving me a trial.

"I can't leave?"

He frowned. "Not until the investigator's finished. He'll be here in two weeks."

We were still nearly four weeks away from Earth; the inspector had to be on some spacecraft speeding toward us.

Unfairness twisted in my gut. Zoe—she should be the one locked up. But was I that different from her? Would I have cut the wires if Dr. Fletcher had asked me to?

I didn't know. But I did know that I'd stayed in the mines to save Cornelius.

"How is my brother?" I asked.

"Recovering."

CHAPTER 24

After Governor Cardoso left, my parents finally got to visit me. Mom hugged me until I thought my spine would snap, then Dad did the same.

"You're safe," Dad whispered, eyes still pinched with concern.

Mom managed a grin. "No broken bones either. Cornelius isn't happy about his arm. No games for him for a while."

"He's awake? He can talk?" I asked, my insides clenching.

"Yes, and complain! Loudly!" Mom laughed.

I sobbed with every muscle in my body. My lungs rattled, my legs shook, and my hands tangled into knots in the sheets. Cornelius was *talking*.

Mom's face fell. "Oh. Oh, sweetheart. I didn't..."

She glanced at Dad for help. He plunked down next to me. "I'm sorry it took us so long to come. We were just making sure Cornelius was all right."

"He's really okay?" I cried. "The lack of oxygen... I thought maybe, there'd be brain damage, or...he wouldn't seem like himself anymore, or..."

"You got him back in time," Dad said. "Give it a few months, and he'll be fine."

My brother was doing even better than I'd dared to hope. I didn't care that I was crying or that my parents were babying me, rubbing my back and murmuring comforting words.

Before Dad left he handed me an extra-large glass with my bar-comp attached.

"For your schoolwork, Ana. I hope you don't fall behind. You've been doing so well." His voice tightened. "I...I know how much your education means to you."

"Just because I was excited about this mission doesn't mean I caused it."

Hope and doubt flickered across my parents' faces. They wanted to believe me, but they couldn't. Not entirely.

"You know we'd still love you even if you did break the shifter, right?" Mom asked.

Nurse Oliveira opened the door. "We covered this. You're not allowed to talk about the sabotage with her, for her own safety."

Both my parents frowned. They hugged me again, told me they still loved me no matter what, then let her escort them away.

All my elation faded into cold sludge at the bottom of my stomach. Even my parents thought I could be a criminal. That I probably was.

After they left, I turned the glass and bar-comp over in my hands. Would the investigator believe me when I told him the truth? I had all the motivation and skills to be the saboteur. I was the obvious culprit.

Queasiness, tiredness, the excitement of Cornelius' recovery... I set my bar-comp on the bedside table.

I slept. Deeply this time. When I woke to my beige cell, I wished I was asleep again, even though fissures and reddish-brown pillars filled my nightmares.

I STAYED IN MY CELL, not that I had a choice. My homework did little to distract me from my thoughts. What could I say to the investigator when he came? I'd been almost as reckless as Zoe, deciding to fix the shifter by myself. Did I deserve to be punished in her place for that?

My parents visited the next day and the day after that. But it was weird only talking about normal things, when nothing was normal about being locked away. Cornelius showed up on the third day after our return, his arm in a splint. He came by himself.

"Hey." He sat on a small aluminum stool. "Thanks. I know I was yelling at you...but I'm pretty sure you saved my life, putting me in all that pain."

Torturing my little brother—one more thing to feel guilty for. He wouldn't have been in danger if I hadn't stayed to repair the shifter. "I'm glad you're alive."

"Me too, even if I'm confined to the hospital until that investigator shows up. Witness and all."

"At least you're not locked in your room."

"Yeah." He smiled weakly, then frowned. "I wish you hadn't cut the wires in the first place. Is Earth really that important to you? I knew you wanted to go, but...but this..."

My throat tightened. How could Cornelius think I'd helped? Didn't he know me better than that?

One of the nurses came in and escorted Cornelius kindly, but firmly, from my room.

No talking about the sabotage. That was the rule.

Had Cornelius not understood Zoe's confession, as muddled as he was? Or had Zoe's story convinced him that he'd heard wrong? I couldn't be upset at Cornelius—everyone else already thought I did it, thanks to Zoe. And they wouldn't let me say otherwise.

Zoe's story was easy to believe. I imagined Dr. Fletcher

asking for my help and guiltily agreeing. Then I envisioned myself going up into the darkness of the mines all alone in the middle of the night, finding the shifter, undoing the star-shaped screws, and slashing through the wires—regret and fear and hope twisting through me. I played it out so many times in my head, it felt almost as real as my memories.

The longer I said nothing, the harder it was to picture myself saying anything when the investigator came. Maybe I deserved to go to jail as much as Zoe did.

Day after day, my only conversations were the stiff ones with my parents or Cornelius. Something sad always lingered around their eyes—like they'd miss me when I moved from this prison to one on Earth.

The hours passed slowly. The nurses wouldn't give me back my wristlet, so I had nothing to do but schoolwork on my bar-comp.

I still fell behind, unable to make myself care. What did school matter when I was going to jail?

The day the investigator arrived felt like the day of my execution.

He entered my hospital-prison and sat on the aluminum stool by my bed. I knew he was the investigator because I didn't recognize him. Not a colony man. He wore a pinstriped suit tailored to his slim, tall frame.

"Hello, Miss Ana Alessandra Pereira Martins. It's a pleasure to meet you. I'm Investigator Alfarsi." He spoke Portuguese cleanly, smoothly, like a doctor assuring a patient that no, this wouldn't hurt very much.

Lies. I rested my hands on top of my blanket and stayed silent.

A frown flickered across his face. "You're...upset about leaving the asteroid? I was told you'd be happy to come to Earth. Cooperative."

"Who'd be happy to go to prison?"

"Prison?" He leaned forward. "Miss Martins, is that what they told you?"

"N-no one's told me anything," I fumbled, feeling stupid.

Investigator Alfarsi nodded. "We needed to keep you safe from threats. I don't know what the accused might do to hide their trail. You're in a position of danger because your testimony is crucial to the case."

"Testimony?"

"You're a minor, Miss Martins. A child who was used and manipulated. You probably consider those who orchestrated the sabotage your friends, but I need you to testify against them."

I gaped. "You're not going to arrest me?"

"No. I need your help—you can point me to the guilty adults. Then I can gather evidence and make some arrests. If I stay to investigate for more than a month, I've signed up for the whole two-year orbit. I'd rather not. I'd like you to come with me and be my key witness."

The past two weeks spun backward. My chest knotted. "This trial... It's on Earth, isn't it?"

"Yes, that's why I thought you'd be cooperative. Who arranged the sabotage?"

He was offering me a ticket to Earth. How many months had I longed for just that? "You're not...taking all the other kids away, right?"

"No, the IC's not classifying this as neglect. We'd rather keep everyone safe by removing the criminals."

I could go to Earth. And the *Platinum Phoenix* wouldn't even be torn apart. I could have everything I'd worked so hard for.

I'd just have to be as underhanded as Zoe. Lie about my actions. Muddle the investigation by pretending I'd been a part of the plot.

I exhaled. Calm ran through me. In that moment, I knew what I would have told Dr. Fletcher if she'd asked me to break the shifter.

"Inspector Alfarsi, I'm afraid there's been a mistake. I'm not the witness you need. But I'd be happy to tell you what I know."

CHAPTER 25

I nspector Alfarsi listened patiently as I related all that had happened, his face blank and unreadable. When I finished, he pursed his lips. "That's an interesting story. I had hoped you'd cooperate."

"I am cooperating. You can check with all the kids, and my dad—Zoe could barely stay awake that morning because she'd been up all night in the mines. She even skipped IDPOP."

"Circumstantial," Investigator Alfarsi muttered. He peered at me, like he was deciding if he should push me further or trust me. "Your brother Cornelius corroborated Zoe's story. He said you confessed to sabotage in the mines."

"Because he was injured and not thinking straight." I wrung the mylar hospital blanket in my hands. I had no evidence, no audio recording. I just had myself...and Zoe's reckless greed.

She'd sabotaged the shifter for a chance to go to Earth. Surely, she'd be eager to give Inspector Alfarsi every detail about Dr. Fletcher's plan—once she knew she wasn't headed to jail.

"Tell Zoe what you told me about being a witness and going to Earth. Then she'll admit she lied about me and get your investigation headed in the right direction."

Inspector Alfarsi returned a day later and let me go. My parents and Cornelius apologized over and over for thinking I could be the saboteur, but I hugged them all fiercely and said I didn't care. I didn't anymore.

I was finally home.

That evening, the hospital returned my wristlet. As soon as I clicked it on, it told me I had two dozen unread messages. At the top of the list was one from Dr. Fletcher.

I opened it. The words projected in blue light over my wrinkled mylar blanket.

Ana,

You've been robbed by forces outside your control. I was so excited for you to attend Mendel. I wanted all the children to have similar opportunities in their lives instead of wasting away and dying with this colony.

That sabotage was supposed to get the IC's attention and it did. I asked Zoe to cut the wires because she wasn't the obvious culprit. I'd hoped that would frustrate and mislead any investigation, drawing it out and forcing the IC to take all the children into protective custody before our next orbit.

Given the way things worked out, maybe I should have asked you to be my saboteur. Or perhaps I should have planned some larger calamity. I'm sorry you're not attending Mendel. I meant every word of the recommendation letter I wrote. You would have made a fine botanist.

Sincerely,
Dr. Fletcher

SHE WAS SORRY ABOUT MENDEL—NOT for hurting us or risking our lives. I felt sick. She hadn't heard Cornelius yelling in the mines or sat in the darkness alone, counting, wondering if he was still breathing.

Dr. Fletcher felt guilty for all the wrong things. She'd sent the apology that let her feel justified—not the one I ought to have. Even if I explained, would she understand what she'd put Cornelius and me through?

I hit the reply button. My fingers hovered over the projected keyboard.

But I didn't owe her a response.

I forwarded her message to the investigator and my parents, then deleted it off my wristlet. Then I blocked her. I didn't need any more letters from Dr. Fletcher.

ZOE ASKED to meet me just before she left with Inspector Alfarsi for Earth. A pair of the guards he'd brought stood on either side of the hallway. Zoe didn't have a bag. Whatever she owned, it would be cheaper to replace it than to bring it.

"Hey." She tucked her hair awkwardly behind her ear. "I'm... sorry. I did, umm, tell the adults what kind of medical help Cornelius needed as soon as my wristlet could transmit, so they'd be there if he made it down. I...I really am glad you're both okay."

The elevator up to the landing bay was right around the corner. In minutes, she'd be gone.

"Me too."

Awkward silence stretched between us. Zoe's voice ached with regret; she meant what she said. If she were apologizing about cheating in a soccer match or breaking my bar-comp, I could have told her it was okay. But it wasn't actually okay that she'd abandoned my brother, and I wasn't going to lie about it. "I hope you like it. Earth, I mean."

Maybe Earth would help her figure out what was really important to her.

Zoe scraped her toe on the floor. "I don't understand why you're letting me go."

I didn't know how to explain.

"You could have had my seat. You'll have to wait at least another orbit now."

"I know." It would have been easy to let everyone keep believing that I was under Dr. Fletcher's thumb—that I could be used.

But *I* didn't want to believe that for the rest of my life.

"When I agreed to sabotage the shifter, I promised Dr. Fletcher I wouldn't say anything, but..." Zoe trailed off. "Do you think it's bad? That I talked with Inspector Alfarsi? I turned Daniel in, too."

Daniel—curly-haired, cheerful Daniel? I felt like I'd swallowed too much algae at once.

"Oh." Zoe tucked her hair back again. "I...thought you knew. You knew about everything else. He wanted his son Lucas to have a chance to get to Earth."

I tried to keep my voice steady around the lump in my throat. "Dr. Fletcher and Daniel knew this could happen. You shouldn't have listened to their plans in the first place."

"They wanted to help me," Zoe said. "Help all of us."

"They almost got Cornelius killed."

Zoe winced. "I know, but..."

She still believed Dr. Fletcher. Or at least half believed her.

"We'll be fine on the asteroid," I said. I'd had a choice to leave, and at least for now, I'd chosen to stay.

"Yeah, good luck with that." Zoe shook her head.

"This place isn't a prison. Or a death trap."

Zoe shrugged. She didn't believe me. "I'm sorry you're not coming. You deserve to."

"No, I don't."

Zoe glanced at the guards. "I wanted to, umm, give you something before I left."

I frowned. Her old mylar clothes? It wasn't like there was a lot of stuff on the asteroid to toss around.

She clicked her wristlet against mine. "There."

"What...was that?"

"The money from my website. After the trial, I'll be living with my aunt, so I won't need it. It's not enough to get you to Earth, but...but I wanted you to have it."

"Th-thanks," I stuttered, surprised.

She gave me a grim smile, a nod, and then turned and walked away—to the elevator, to the waiting shuttle, to Earth. To all the things she'd hoped to gain through sabotage.

And what did I have? A brother who loved me. And I knew what kind of person I was. Two things I wanted more than everything on Earth.

I walked away slowly. After so much time in the hospital, my legs still felt cramped. I felt cramped, tired—inside and out.

My wristlet flashed. I half expected an accusation of stealing Zoe's money, but instead, it displayed a message from Governor Cardoso: "All non-essential personnel, including children, please report immediately to the recreation hall for an announcement."

Strange. I turned the other way. The corridors soon filled with people whispering, wondering. I strode alongside the crowd, eventually finding Dad, Mom, and Cornelius. Chairs formed neat rows, just like at the mission vote—except there were a lot more chairs.

Next to the podium sat a large table with a giant cake on it. A *real cake*. Seven tiers tall, covered in thick, yellow frosting. There were piles of foils with the bright orange labels used only for sweet juices, too.

"What do you think the cake's for?" Cornelius whispered.

I shook my head. "I don't know, but the inspector must have brought us some supplies on his shuttle."

There hadn't been any sugar or wheat on board for months, and the supply shipment from the Lunar Colonies wouldn't come for at least another week.

Cornelius turned to Dad. "Can we...can we go look at it, a bit closer? We'll come back when the speaking starts."

"Just wait," Dad said. He grinned. Hugely. And he didn't look surprised at all.

A hundred other similar conversations swirled around us —*Cake! Why? What for?*—but it all turned to silence the second Governor Cardoso stood and stepped up to the podium. He tapped his wristlet and waited as it calculated which language had the largest percentage of fluent speakers present.

He continued in Portuguese. "Thank you all for gathering to our impromptu celebration. First, I would like to announce that those behind the sabotage in the mines have been arrested and removed from the asteroid. Ana and Cornelius Martins have fully recovered from their ordeal and have been released from the hospital."

He said that like we'd had pneumonia or something, glossing over the botched mission that put us there and my imprisonment. He made no effort to apologize for his false accusations either. But I didn't need Governor Cardoso's praise, and the applause ringing through the hall sounded nice.

"Now, for the announcement we've called you here for. Dr. Kim, would you stand?"

I'd been too focused on the frosting to notice Dr. Kim sitting with the board members near the podium.

"Dr. Kim's excellent aeroponics work has contributed to drought relief and water management efforts on Earth, garnering quite some attention. I am pleased to announce that this morning, *seven* different countries and organizations approved research grants."

I jumped to my feet and clapped and shouted. So did everyone else. We sounded like a stampede.

Governor Cardoso smiled, waiting for the commotion to die down. "We have accordingly ordered a new 3-D fabricator, as well as a smaller-sized back-up capable of manufacturing replacement parts for the main fab, should anything happen to it. People are taking an interest in us again—in space and what it can offer. Who knows? Perhaps they'll even start building the space elevator again one day." He chuckled at his own joke. "But enough of speeches. I know you're all really here to eat cake. Form lines on both sides, please."

Cake, a backup fab, and grants. It seemed surreal.

Cornelius and I made our way toward the line, but a quiet voice stopped me. "Ah, Ana."

I turned and saw Dr. Kim. She clasped her hands behind her back. "I'm glad to hear you'll be continuing with us."

"Thanks."

"With these new grants, I'm tripling the size of aeroponics. I'm going to need plenty of help testing new crops. One of our grants named cotton a priority. The Lunar Colonies is sending us seeds. I'm quite pleased about it. If we're successful, you won't be stuck in those mylar rags for much longer."

Real clothes. I wouldn't mind that.

Dr. Kim continued. "I've requested that you be allowed to do IDPOP in aeroponics every afternoon to help with that project specifically."

I stared. "Really?"

Botany, every day. Botany that mattered—both to the asteroid and Earth.

"We did just lose a botanist. This is real work, Ana. You'll have to work hard. But I think," she said, "you can handle a challenge."

"Th-thank you," I stammered.

"1300 sharp. Tomorrow. You'll be getting the units prepped for planting." She said that like it was routine, ordinary. Then someone on the board cut in, and she walked away to talk about grants.

Dr. Kim was nicer than I'd given her credit for. Excitement whirled in my head. It wasn't the Pampas, but aeroponics every afternoon? Shelf after shelf of my own plants? Important, real experiments? It wasn't the future I'd planned, but it still sounded amazing.

Cornelius and I each grabbed the biggest piece of cake we could wheedle out of the servers. The inside was fluffy white, with a layer of lemon curd. We sat against the wall, our feet out, nibbling to savor every morsel.

Even once the cake was gone, we kept running our fingers over our plates, hoping to catch some lingering trace of frosting.

"I thought you were going to leave," he said.

"I didn't cut those wires."

He licked his finger. "You still could have gone."

"But I didn't."

Maybe I'd go to Earth one day. Or maybe I'd live here forever. I wasn't sure anymore. I was just glad that for now, I'd chosen to stay.

After extracting every last atom of sweetness off my plate, I set it down. "Want to play *Penguin Mountain?*"

"Umm?" Cornelius nodded at his arm in the sling.

I got up and sat on the other side of him, by his good arm.

"There. I'll project it off of my wristlet—" I pulled it up "—and we can both play."

Cornelius grinned. I watched him laugh as the penguin crashed. He wasn't any good left-handed, but that didn't matter. I laughed along with him—just like we used to.

People stayed in the rec hall chatting and laughing long past our bedtimes. Cornelius and I played ten more games, ate second slices of cake, and got dragged into a soccer game with Dae-sung and Jayden.

A new 3-D fab. Grant money. Aeroponics. Those words buzzed around us. Zoe was wrong about the *Platinum Phoenix.* It wasn't a death trap. It wasn't dying.

It was being reborn. And I'd be here to help it grow.

ACKNOWLEDGMENTS

This book has a long history. I will invariably forget someone, and I apologize in advance. I first started writing this novel in 2013 after playing a few too many games of *High Frontier*—and then thinking about situations in which a young protagonist could take center stage even with responsible, involved adults in her life. That book became a short story and now has come full-circle back into a novel.

I didn't realize before I started making a list just how many people read and gave their insights and comments on this book. Much thanks goes to Kindal Debenham, Emily Hamblin Debenham, Ailsa Lillywhite, Evan Witt, Andy Lemmon, Ben Hardin, John Hutchins, Carolyn Duede, Michelle Cowart, Matt Brown, Laurel Amberdine, and J.S. Bangs. David Dunton, thank you for your comments and enthusiasm for this book, too.

Cast of Wonders published a short story created from the beginning of this book, also entitled "Ana's Asteroid". Marguerite Kenner worked on getting that short story polished and ready for production, and Alethea Kontis preformed the audio. Thank you both for bringing that slice of Ana's story to life.

And then there are so many fabulous people at Immortal Works who have made the book you are reading a reality. Beth Buck, Holli Anderson, Julia King, Jason King, Ruth Mitchell, Katie Lewis, and Staci Olsen—thank you. I need to give an extra shout-out to Rebecca Barney who designed the cover. It is always a never-wracking moment as an author to see what's going on the front of your novel, but when I saw the artwork, I felt like *Ana's Asteroid* was a real book instead of this thing that I'd kept on my computer for far too long.

Lastly, I want to thank my family. I feel incredibly lucky to have such a supportive extended family as well as a loving husband and four of the most amazing children on any planet. I love you all.

ABOUT THE AUTHOR

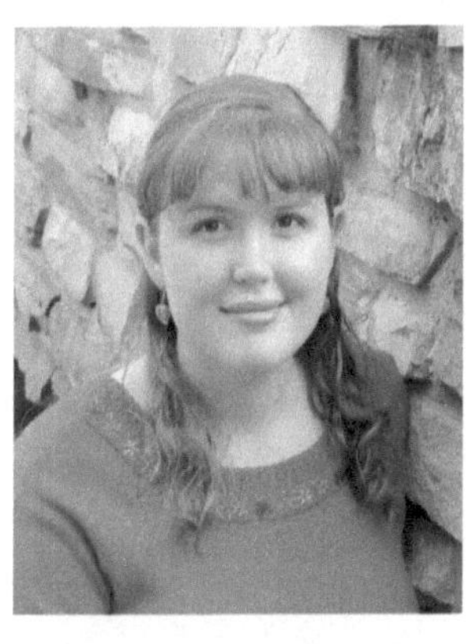

M.K. Hutchins often draws on her background in archaeology when writing fantasy and science fiction. She's the author of the YA fantasy novels *The Redwood Palace, The Coral Palace,* and *Drift,* along with over thirty short stories appearing in *Podcastle, Analog, Strange Horizons,* and elsewhere. When not writing, she's usually with her children as they grow veggies, bake, read books, and play board games together, though not usually all at the same time. Find her at www.mkhutchins.com.

This has been an
Immortal Production